I0520335

GEORGE ELLIS

40+

First edition

ISBN: 978-1-7364843-3-3

Cover art by Rob Story

This book was professionally typeset on Reedsy.
Find out more at reedsy.com

Contents

Chapter 1

Exactly 14,610 days after he was born, my best friend died. Just like everyone does.

The funeral lasted three hours, and true to form, Paul was fall-down drunk when the moment of truth finally came. A lot of people choose to die lying down, perhaps in a nice casket or on their own bed. Hammocks have been fashionable the last few years. Paul collapsed on stage, in the middle of a sloppy guitar solo he'd taught himself for just the occasion. There he was, in front of his friends and family at a midrate banquet hall in suburban Chicago, sweating and jumping and playing his bright-blue axe. Then, plop. Down like a fish he went. His face slammed into the wooden planks, producing a fleshy thud. It sounded like someone slapped the floor with a fistful of lunchmeat.

He was dead before he landed.

Paul chose to go out playing music because he thought it would help him lose track of the final seconds. You know, make it more of a surprise. But just before his heart stopped beating, he looked at me and winked. There was no surprise. He knew the moment was upon him, the same as everyone else in the room did, even without the benefit of glancing at his watch. It was cruel. Not only was his death inescapable, but the knowledge of it was too. As the last few echoes of his electric guitar reverberated against the walls, Paul's sister turned to me and smiled.

"I still have time to learn an instrument. Maybe I'll die that way too," she said.

Marisa was thirty-four, six years younger than Paul and therefore six years away from her own expiration date. She was a smart woman, and she shared Paul's belief that life was too short to waste on fleeting things like accomplishments. She had worked as a waitress from ages thirteen to thirty, and currently spent most of her free time as a retiree traveling the world. I'd known her for half her life. When I was in my late twenties, we often had sex. It never turned into anything serious. Neither of us wanted a relationship or kids, but we were both middle-aged and attractive, so why not?

Per his wishes, we moved Paul into a throne on the stage, propped an old fashioned in his hand, and continued his funeral for another couple hours, drinking way too much as we memorialized our late friend. We traded stories of his life and mused about our own deaths. Most of the attendees were at least thirty, so we all had the big 4-0 on our minds. If not in the forefront, always there in the shadows. Lurking. Biding its time and tipping the scales on every decision we made. The closer each of us got to the end, the more death would rule our thoughts, no matter how hard we tried to ignore it.

Eventually, everyone had filed out of the banquet hall except for me and Marisa. We said our goodbyes to Paul, nodded to the teenaged funeral director, and walked outside into the warm summer night. The venue was located in a strip mall. Paul had spent the last of his money on the best guitar he could find, meaning he had to skimp on the funeral and hold it in the burbs, as opposed to Lakeview, the trendy area of Chicago where we lived.

Marisa and I looked at each other in the parking lot. A breeze caught her blonde hair and pushed a few wispy strands past her eyes. I reached over and tucked her bangs behind her ear.

My car had a bigger back seat than hers, so we had sex there.

Afterward, as she walked away, I knew I'd never see her again. I was 14,585 days old, after all, and had more important plans before the end than hanging out with my dead best friend's sister, as pleasant as she was.

I thought about Paul a lot the next day. We'd shared a two-bedroom apartment for nearly fifteen years. Aside from a few spans here and there when one of us had other places to be—my year in Germany or his short-lived marriage in Ohio, for example—Paul and I had basically become a platonic couple. He was my life partner. Now he was gone, along with all his possessions. Paul was the middle child, and Marisa was his only living sibling; she had come by a week earlier to collect some sentimental items, and then he and I sold or donated the rest.

I relaxed on the couch and flipped through the channels, not really watching anything. It was the weekend. For the last few years, Paul and I had a tradition of ordering pizza and then hitting up our local bar every Saturday night. Whoever found a love connection first had rights to the apartment, and the other agreed to spend the evening in the cheap motel across the street. More often than not, we both ended up at the apartment. The closer we got to forty, finding a partner became increasingly difficult, if only by imperceptible amounts. Hell, Marisa might have merely been taking pity on me in the back of my car after Paul's funeral.

I opened the fridge and had to smile. One of my pet peeves of having Paul as my roommate was his habit of leaving half-eaten sandwiches and snacks in the fridge, along with open cans of soda he hadn't quite finished. Somehow, on the day of his death, he'd found time to hide a dozen items in the fridge in various states of decay or destruction. The thought of him hurriedly taking bites of whatever he could find and then stuffing it in the fridge while I waited down in the car was hilarious. He'd even taken the time to arrange the gross cornucopia so it was blocking anything of my own I might actually want to eat. There was a note stuck to what was left of a cupcake: "Got ya, fucker."

And he did get me. I mean, how was I going to get him back for that? I couldn't. Except by eating the food just to spite him. So, that's exactly what I did. I grabbed a mangled bologna sandwich and an open, flat can of soda and walked to the couch.

"Got ya back, jerk," I said between bites.

If I could somehow stomach finishing most of his leftovers, I reasoned, I was pretty sure that would put me on top for good. I was so pleased with myself that I didn't notice the son of a bitch had slipped raspberry jam in the sandwich. I was allergic to raspberries, meaning the next few hours were going to be full of wheezing and hives. I raised my can of pop to the sky, then to the floor just in case, and toasted the bastard. He had got me after all.

Chapter 2

McGee's was more crowded than usual, meaning instead of two empty stools on either side of me at the bar, I had just one. Other than New Year's Eve, I'd never seen the place more than a third full. It was one of those establishments that was part Irish pub, part sports bar, and all dive. Even on the weekends, it was mostly just the locals. The lingering stench of cigarette smoke hung in the air and mixed with the smell of stale peanuts. I felt the familiar crackle of empty shells under my feet as I scraped the stool closer to the bar. Mark arrived with a pint of amber ale, my usual for the start of the night. He looked at the empty spot next to me and sighed.

"Did he rock it until the end?" Mark asked.

Mark owned McGee's. Just twenty-two, he had inherited the pub the year before from his father. Come to think of it, that night was the most packed I'd ever seen the place. We had all gathered around for one last evening of revelry with Stan McGee himself. The guy had timed up his death to be the moment he downed a shot of whiskey. He placed his glass on the table, then settled back into the corner booth and closed his eyes, seemingly in one fluid motion. It was a good way to go.

"He was melting everyone's faces off," I said, referring to Paul's guitar solo the night before. I raised the shot of whiskey that Mark had delivered with the beer and clinked it with the shot in his hand.

"To Paul, the whiniest customer I ever had the pleasure of serving," Mark toasted. We both drank.

"That he was," I agreed, exhaling. Paul had a habit of complaining about the tiniest thing wrong with his drink, from a smudge on the glass to a little too much foam on the head. It played into the old-man stereotype, but he'd been that way since he was twenty.

"You should tell me your beer is skunked, just to honor his legacy," joked Mark. "Either way, that one's on the house, old-timer."

As I watched Mark move to the very drunk guy at the end of the bar and negotiate a trade—another drink for his car keys—it struck me that my exchange with Mark about Paul's picky manner might just be the last time I spoke of Paul out loud with anyone. We shared no other friends. I'd already slept with his sister one last time. And with that silence, poof. He would be erased from existence. I pulled out my phone and checked his Facebook profile. There was a smattering of comments and heart emojis from the night before, and Facebook had automatically updated his profile status to expired. It was now locked in place for all eternity with a photo of Paul on stage, sweat glistening on his brow and a smile plastered on his face.

"This seat taken?" a woman asked, her perfume covering me like a heavy blanket as she slid onto the stool next to me. She used makeup as liberally as perfume, but she was an attractive woman, with brown eyes and dark, curly hair to match. Her shirt was practically painted on, accentuating a slender, sexy frame. She smiled at me, then nodded to Mark.

"Tequila," she said, before motioning to my pint glass. "That any good?"

I nodded.

"One of those to chase it," she added.

I sipped my beer and turned my attention back to the TV. It was mid-June, and the Cubs were on their way to the playoffs again. When I was a kid, they couldn't escape the cellar. My mom would take me to a few games a year at Wrigley. I think they won twice. For the last decade, however, they'd finally lived up to their big market expectations, making the postseason nearly every year. I hadn't been to a game since last season, but if they were on TV while I was at McGee's, I was happy for the diversion.

"Ugh, men and their sports. I never understood the love affair," the woman said to no one in particular. Well, she was talking to me, but she was looking at herself in the mirror over the bar. I turned to meet her eyes in the reflection.

"I'm Dana," she offered.

"William."

"Don't let me distract you from those men running around in circles for no reason," she joked.

"Diamonds, actually," I said.

Dana turned to get a good look at me. "It's a figure of speech, Bill. Can I call you Bill?"

"Sure."

"I like William. It's a nice name. But you look more like a Bill to me. And anyway, I realize that it's a baseball diamond, not a baseball circle. But for all intents and purposes, they're running in circles. If you're gonna argue with me about that, it kind of makes you an asshole."

"I don't want to be one of those."

"I had a feeling you didn't. Just to be sure, maybe you should buy my next drink."

That caught me off guard. I mean, I wouldn't say I'm an unattractive guy. Women have always liked me just fine. But this felt ... staged somehow. Weird in a way that I couldn't quite put my finger on.

"Or don't. Up to you, asshole," she added.

I laughed and motioned for Mark to get another round for both of us.

"You smoke?" she asked, offering a cigarette.

I took one. She produced a lighter and sparked mine first, then hers. Mark dropped an ashtray off as he passed by.

"So, what's a relatively average-looking guy like you doing all alone in a bar on a Saturday night?" Dana asked. "I don't see any major problems on the surface."

"I guess mine run deeper," I replied, trying to figure out her angle. Maybe she was working? I felt like a dick even considering that, but it was more a compliment than a judgment. She was attractive and witty. Why was she set on chatting me up? "What about you?"

"Oh, I've got all sorts of problems. I don't want to bore you."

"Please, go ahead."

"There are the obvious ones. Drinking. Drugs. Fear of commitment. And on top of all that, I'm lactose intolerant, so I can't eat ice cream or pizza. I could go on."

"I think I get the picture," I said. I liked her. I was a sucker for blunt women. Which only made me even more skeptical.

"You're wondering why I'm bothering you," she interjected.

"Not bothering ..."

"That's a start."

She stubbed out her smoke and flicked her eyes at the TV,

then smirked. The Cubs had just lost on a walk-off homer.

"You were saying?" I prompted.

"Maybe I'm lonely too."

"I never said I was lonely."

"We're all lonely, Bill," she said. But she knew I wasn't buying it. She sighed and put her hands up in mock surrender. "I'm kind of a fan."

Ah. The book.

About ten years ago, I had a brief flirtation with being a writer. My day job was working in advertising as an art director. Since I was about to turn thirty at the time, my career was coming to an end. Nobody wanted ideas from an old person, especially not in the advertising field. You hit thirty or thirty-one, and you were forced out. It started innocently enough with a few meetings or assignments you wouldn't be included on. A new kids product? Bill probably wouldn't understand. A cool beer brand targeted at twenty-one-year-olds? Don't get the old guy! Put him on the funeral services or toothpaste account. Then, they ask you to mentor a new person right out of junior college. A few months after that, if you haven't taken the hint and gracefully shown yourself the door, they'll find a reason. Cutbacks. Redundancies. They had plenty of ways to skin that cat.

With diminishing responsibilities at work, I began writing at night. It was the year Paul was off playing house with that ill-chosen wife in Ohio. Basically, I was bored. That's how it started anyway. The next thing I knew, I'd quit my job and was spending all day in front of the computer, chain-smoking and writing a novel. I had no idea what I was doing, which actually worked in my favor. When I submitted the manuscript to agents, they said it was raw and unfiltered, with "little regard for pretense." It ended up being published a year later and garnered a small cult following, mostly composed of women in their twenties and thirties who found the main character refreshingly honest. In the foreword, I'd mentioned that much of the research for the book had been done at McGee's. That resulted in a few women tracking me down here. The last time had been years ago, however, so Dana surprised me.

"I'm not a stalker or anything," she said.

"No, you just tracked me down based on something I wrote ten years ago. Perfectly normal."

Dana's eyes met mine again as she tried to determine if I was serious. I shrugged.

"You live nearby?" she asked.

* * *

Dana closed the fridge door and looked at me with alarm. "I suddenly feel very worried about the fact I'm not wearing shoes."

"Or underwear," I noted, glancing at her bare legs. She instinctively pulled the T-shirt she'd borrowed from my closet a little further down to cover herself and eyed the front door.

"I can explain," I said. "All that half-eaten food isn't mine."

"Is that supposed to make me feel better? You live with some kind of deranged food hoarder?"

By the time I'd coaxed her into the living room and explained the situation to her, Dana agreed that Paul had, in fact, scored a decisive victory.

"I kind of wish I'd slept with him instead," she said. "Sounds like he was a funny guy."

"He didn't like women with bad attitudes and curly hair."

Dana leaned back into me on the couch and flicked her hand playfully at my face. "That's very specific. And my hair isn't naturally curly. Do you ever wish you decided to go the family route?"

We were watching a shitty rom-com about a twenty-five-year-old bachelor who inherits three kids from his sister who died in a plane crash.

"Nope," I said.

Dana slid the remote out of my hand and flipped the channels. She paused briefly on a reality show about fashion designers, then saw the look on my face and kept going. "You can't handle me driving the remote, can you?"

"I'm fine with it," I said half-heartedly. "Want another donut?"

"Sure."

I went to the kitchen, leaving her to (hopefully) pick something good to watch. It surprised me that she wanted to stay and hang out. For the past few years, sex had been mainly transactional for me. Maybe she didn't have anywhere else to stay. She hadn't asked for money, so I was fairly sure my working-girl theory was incorrect. That was good. But she also seemed a bit too normal given how quickly we'd jumped into bed together. My book definitely wasn't *that* good. I dropped two donuts on a plate and walked back into the living room, where Dana was watching the news.

"Bummer," I said. "I was hoping for an action movie or maybe—"

Dana shushed me and turned up the volume on the TV. As I sat down on the couch, I saw the breaking news chyron scrolling at the bottom of the screen. I tried to offer Dana her donut, but she ignored me.

"Authorities have confirmed the unidentified man's date of

birth and are still gathering details at this time," the news anchor reported with a sense of urgency normally reserved for natural disasters or international military conflicts. "A spokesperson for the hospital in Atlanta is currently speaking to the media."

As they cut to a serious woman in a pantsuit standing among a gaggle of reporters in a media briefing room, I took a closer look at the ticker on the television: CONFIRMED: GEORGIA MAN 14,612 DAYS OLD.

"Holy shit," I said.

Dana nodded. "Yeah."

We watched the press conference in stunned silence. The woman was the director of Grady Memorial Hospital in central Atlanta. What she had to say was shocking: a day earlier, a local man had checked himself into the hospital, claiming he had lived past forty years of age. Claims like that are not uncommon, she said. It apparently happens to people who either grew up in the care of the state and somehow had a mistake in their records, or the individual is simply seeking attention. However, in this case, the man, who she would only refer to as Patient K, had also been born at Grady Memorial forty years earlier, so they were able to track down his records and confirm his age.

According to Patient K's eldest daughter, the man's funeral had been planned for months. He was supposed to expire at exactly 7:32 p.m. But when the time came, he just lay there in his casket. Awake. Breathing. The family waited until the next day before convincing Patient K to go to the hospital.

I didn't realize my hands were shaking until I felt Dana put her own hand atop one of mine. She continued to look at the TV. The hospital director was finishing her briefing.

"His vitals are normal, and we aren't seeing any indications that he has suffered trauma of any sort," she said. "Obviously, we will continue to monitor him very closely, and we are already working with experts from the National Institutes of Health and the federal government, who have been extremely gracious in their collaboration."

The doctor paused, then looked into the TV cameras, knowing the gravity of the moment.

"If this is not an isolated case, we all understand the implications of Patient K's condition. Our doctors will do their very best to give this man the finest care possible, while also determining what has caused him to outlive his expiration date. Thank you."

The gallery of reporters immediately erupted with questions, but the director smiled tersely and walked past the row of men and women who had been standing at attention behind her, no doubt the highest-level doctors on staff. A press agent for the NIH replaced her at the podium and began providing a series of non-answers, not wanting to offer any more information—or perhaps he just didn't have any.

Still dazed by the news, I took the remote from Dana and turned the TV down from its max volume to something more tolerable. For about a minute, we just sat there, side by side, listening to the press agent's talking points.

"Well fuck a duck," Dana finally said, taking her donut from the plate on the couch. She raised it to her mouth, then considered it. "Guess I might have to start watching my cholesterol after all."

I snorted out a laugh. I had no idea of her exact age, but it was likely somewhere sub-thirty-five, based on the lack of wrinkles around her eyes. She turned to me, and I could see the question coming before she voiced it.

"Thirty-eight," I lied.

Why I lied, I wasn't sure. If anything, news that post 4-0 was possible should have made me happy. Sure, if the guy was legit, he probably only represented a one-in-a-billion shot, but that still meant it was technically possible.

"Thirty-eight and five months," I added, thinking that if I was more specific, it might lend credence to the lie.

Dana nodded, but I could tell she didn't believe me. Something triggered in her mind, and I knew the laid-back camaraderie we'd been enjoying all evening was gone. She stood up awkwardly.

"I think I'm gonna go," she said, her mind already a million miles away.

"Of course. Yeah. Totally," I said.

She looked at me and then seemed to snap back into the moment. She smiled warmly, and there was sadness in her eyes. It almost seemed like regret. "I had a good time," she said. "I'm … sorry. But I really do have to go. I have surgery in the morning."

"You're a surgeon?"

"What? You're surprised?"

"Honestly, yeah. I didn't really get surgeon coming from you."

"If it makes you feel better, the patient is a German shepherd. Removing a few rotten teeth. And I'm just assisting. Vet tech."

"Working with animals. That I can see."

A few minutes later, she was back in her own clothes, and I was opening the door for her. She said she didn't need a ride. Once she stepped into the hall, Dana paused and turned back. She was about to say something, then just walked away instead. It was an odd end to a pleasant encounter, but to be honest, I was relieved she was gone. I felt too charged to be around anyone else, let alone a virtual stranger.

After forty.

I knew I wouldn't be sleeping much tonight. So, instead of getting ready for bed, I grabbed a six-pack of beer and plopped back down on the couch to watch the twenty-four-hour news channels hyperventilate about the "miracle man" in Atlanta. For once, I didn't think they were being sensational. For thousands of years, humans had been dropping dead exactly 14,610 days after they were born. Men. Women. Healthy. Sick. No exceptions.

Until this guy. I couldn't decide if he was an asshole or a hero.

About half of the commentators thought it was a hoax or a clerical error on the part of the hospital. It was hard to blame them. Billions of people had succumbed to forty before this Patient K came along and simply … kept living. And with each additional second that passed, he flouted the natural order of things on an even deeper level. He could die at any moment, and he still had changed the course of history. If two days was possible, why not two weeks? Or two years?

Two decades.

I looked at the recliner next to the couch. For years, Paul had sat in that spot, watching TV with me. If only he were here to see this.

Chapter 3

A week passed. I now had just nineteen days to live. Probably.

Not only was Patient K still alive, five other people across the globe had crossed the Rubicon into forty-plus territory. Four women and another man. Only one of them was an American; she was an actor from Los Angeles who had been in a few horror movies in her twenties. She was suddenly a thousand times more famous, thanks to merely staying alive longer than expected. The other "forty-somethings," as people started calling them, were from various parts of the world. A fisherman from South America. An accountant from France. There were no connections, and seemingly no pattern to explain why any of them were outlasting the rest of us.

To say these people rocked the world would be an understatement.

In addition to the media frenzy, the global financial markets were apoplectic, with health stocks skyrocketing from Wall Street to Tokyo. The idea that people might live longer and need more care had investors rushing to cash in on the possibilities. Not every sector was so lucky. The expiration industry cratered, despite only six people out of a few billion lasting longer than expected. Funeral parlors, banquet halls, last-trip companies, they were all hit hard. Tobacco companies took it on the chin. I hadn't touched a cigarette since the news first broke. It was silly, really. I had about a one-in-a-billion chance of seeing the sun rise on day 14,611. But there I was, walking to the convenience mart to pick up a six-pack of light beer. Not regular beer. No. The light stuff. Easier on the waistline, which was in turn easier on the blood pressure, according to my internet research. I was even considering buying some vitamins or pomegranate juice or something, if the place wasn't out of stock. It probably was.

I clearly wasn't alone in my delusion. Everywhere I went, I saw that same glimmer of hope in other people's eyes. Mostly the elderly, like me. The overweight, had-to-be-close-to-forty guy at the grocery store stocking up on fruit. The retirees sporting brand-new workout attire, trying to learn how the weight machines at the gym functioned. If their expiration dates didn't kill them, dropping dead of a heart attack after like twelve minutes on the treadmill might. In a convenient twist, my advanced age helped me skip the regular line and head straight to the first open checkout counter to score a few more items before they sold out. One of the perks of being over thirty-eight. Well, that and the 50 percent discount at the movie theater. It didn't quite make up for the worst parts of aging, like wrinkles or hair where you didn't want hair, but it was something.

On my walk home from the convenience mart, I passed a pair of late teens getting into an Uber, their suitcases in tow, no doubt heading to the airport to set off on some sun-drenched, globetrotting adventure. They didn't have a care in the world—or that was my read of the situation as a guy less than a few weeks from never having anything left in the world, let alone a care. Fucking teens. Being that young should be

17

illegal.

Seeing them reminded me that I was supposed to be in Hawaii. That had been my plan all along: spend the last three weeks enjoying a tropical getaway, wicking away at my meager nest egg until it hit zero, just as my time ran out. But once the news of the forty-somethings hit, I skipped the flight. Instead of planning for the inevitable, I had become obsessed with the possibility of forty-plus, meaning my finances needed to be ready for that contingency as well. Thankfully, I didn't have to notify anybody about my change in itinerary. My best friend was dead. I had no living family, and my friends all thought I was still a year away from expiration.

Yeah ... so there's that little nugget.

A lot of people lie about their age, only telling their closest friends and relatives their exact day count, but I'd taken things a step further. My father expired when I was eighteen, my mother a year earlier, and I realized with no other relatives to speak of, nobody knew my real age. Except the government, obviously. Having just seen what my father went through in his final days—the endless procession of friends and coworkers offering hollow sympathies—I decided I wanted to end things on my own terms. Alone. So, from that moment forward, I told everybody I was exactly eight months younger than I was. I didn't even tell Paul my real age until about a week before his own expiration. (He thought it was funny.)

Given the new reality, I couldn't be happier with the choice to hide my real age. Now, I could still die alone if I wanted to, but I could also live in anonymity for a while if I happened to exceed my expiration. No press conferences. No doctors drawing countless vials of blood to determine my body's secret. Just me and my longevity.

If it happened.

I didn't really believe it would.

Or did I?

I wasn't so sure anymore. What I *was* sure about is my decision not to undergo suppression therapy. Also known as age gapping, the process involved having your earliest memories suppressed. Only two companies were licensed to perform the procedure. It was outrageously expensive and somewhat risky; 3 percent of the people who underwent the therapy woke up with various degrees of memory loss from their entire life, not just the early years. The idea was simple. Your birthday is one of your earliest memories. If it is removed, you don't know your exact age. While you're at the facility undergoing the procedure, the company has a team of digital and in-person staff erasing your age from your house, your files, your computer—even your health records. Once the process is complete, only the government knows your exact age. Oh sure, your friends and family would as well, but almost everyone who goes through the therapy is unattached. Being suppressed means you have about a six-month window of when you *could* die. This ambiguity is supposed to be freeing and allow you to have some sense of spontaneity in your death, for lack of a better word.

Point is, I'm glad I didn't do it. I wanted to know the exact days now. Needed to know them.

The other thing I needed to know was what happened to the human body after forty years of age. I was not alone in this quest for information. In the short time since Patient K arrived on the scene, talk of post-expiration health dominated the media (and rightfully so, it could be argued). Talk shows. Cable news. Podcasts. The most qualified professionals such as doctors and age specialists seemed to be the most reserved in their hypotheses, and because of that were drowned in the cacophony of blustery claims by pundits, politicians, and quacks. Most people agreed that the body would slowly deteriorate the first few months and years post-forty, but what happened after that was quite literally anybody's guess.

Nobody had ever lived it before.

One popular theory was that all your bones would break before you turned fifty. Just grind into dust! Fractures and breaks were certainly more common the more you aged, due to decreased bone density, and assuming an increase in bone deterioration coupled with that problem, the idea seemed to have some merit. It was certainly less far-fetched than the prediction put forth by one guest on the *Tonight Show* who claimed organs would liquify the moment a person turned forty-four. Her rationale for this? She cited the time she cooked chicken liver.

Hair loss. Blindness. Exponentially increased blood pressure. Giant noses. Second menopause. Reverse menopause. Weird spots on the skin caused by the liver. Constipation to the point of a ruptured large intestine. Confusion. Total and complete loss of memory. Also, total and complete loss of bladder control. And motor function.

Inability to achieve an erection. Ever. If your penis didn't fall right off, which was a theory making the rounds on the internet.

Loss of appetite after 6 p.m.

I was both horrified and fascinated as I sat there, day after day, glued to the TV. Or, if I was in the bathroom, frantically scrolling on my phone. Medical websites initially crashed, then began to reap the millions of dollars in ad revenue from all the traffic. Within a week, the FCC had to regulate how much money a health-related website could make per day on Google ads. It was still a lot, if the health stocks were any indication.

I did my best to absorb the opinions and predictions, but I was simply overwhelmed by the sheer amount of information. They had turned on the fire hose, and I was standing directly in front of it. One moment I would be making a list of the best foods to eat (fucking berries, I knew it!), and the next I was on the couch, dazed, trying to slow down my heart rate with a breathing exercise because a social media influencer said the fewer beats your heart creates, the longer it will last. Which made sense!

The heart.

That was the key!

It had been mysteriously and reliably shutting down at exactly the same moment (14,610 days) for millennia. That was no longer the case. If you could just keep the heart going, everything else would follow. But you had to solve the heart first.

Fewer beats. Less butter. More breathing. Well, not more breathing, just more relaxed breathing. More sleep? Does the heart rate slow down during sleep? I Googled that. Yes, it does. So, all I had to do to live longer was sleep more. I could totally manage that. Usually. The stress of the current situation was actually making it hard to sleep more than three or four hours a night, which made me angry at myself, which in turn made it even harder to sleep. It was a vicious cycle that was going to cost me in the end, I decided.

Chapter 4

If the first week of this new era was all about shocking the global system into a new reality, the second week was when the wheels came off. Like the brittle bones of a hypothetical forty-seven-year-old, society began to crack.

Large swaths of the global workforce quit. You'd think the prospect of needing to maintain your job longer than before would motivate people to work harder, but you'd be wrong. Reason did not apply. Most humans were, like me, obsessed with the possibilities. Instead of staying the course, they wondered what it would be like to veer into uncharted territory. For years, the general age of retirement had hovered around thirty-three, but now the entire idea of retirement seemed obsolete. Or something that could be put off for years. Decades? What if the new lifespan wasn't forty-two or forty-three, but sixty. Or seventy!

The mere thought of a human body still being able to function at eighty—double the current expiration age—was as exhilarating as it was horrifying. By eighty, I had no doubt limbs and genitals would be falling off.

As someone who was already retired, I didn't have to quit my job. And there was no use looking for new employment—even with the current developments, no companies were interested in hiring anybody past the age of thirty-seven. I just had to find a way to preoccupy myself for another twelve days without losing my mind.

I also had to find a way to disappear, thanks to the newly created Expiration Task Force, the ETF. Operating as an enforcement arm of the Department of Health and Human Services, the ETF had a simple mission: track down anybody whose expiration date had passed, but who had not been admitted to a morgue. They were looking for the proverbial needle in a haystack, and they had already found one man, a farmer in Iowa, who was a full three days past his expiration. He'd been hiding out in his barn, nervous about the attention he would receive (understandable) and the things the government planned to do to his body (even more understandable). The ETF claimed that for the greater good, all forty-somethings had a civic duty to notify authorities and undergo a series of "noninvasive" tests and procedures. The exact nature of these tests was unclear, though it seemed ol' Iowa Farmer Guy was on the right track when he tried to hide. Anytime the words greater good get trotted out as a reason for a governmental agency to act, it's usually for the greater bad for the individual in their crosshairs.

The fact that the ETF found one person seemed to indicate that there could be hundreds out there. The official global count was sixty-four. I had no plans on being test subject sixty-five. It was a scenario I hadn't planned for. I had successfully thrown my friends off my trail so I could die on my own terms, but the government still knew my exact birthdate. It was in the same database as every single other American citizen's exact time and place of birth. Before the ETF, nobody was hunting down missing expired people. They just were found or not found. No biggie.

My first thought was to buy another pair of tickets to Hawaii, but not only was that trackable, new restrictions were in place for anyone more than 14,550 days old. It seems all interstate and international plane travel had to be reviewed and approved by the ETF. Due to the immediate backlog, however, you might have to wait two to three months for approval. Meaning you'd be dead by the time you were allowed to board the plane. Or train. Or bus, in theory. (I kinda doubted they were checking all the bus tickets, but anything is possible.)

Luckily, they couldn't stop a person from driving.

So. Where to go? Since I lived in Chicago, I was pretty much smack-dab in the middle of the country. I could be in Colorado by the morning. As I considered my options, there was a knock at the door. It was probably my neighbor Ted again. Just about every other day since the news broke, he'd been stopping by to rant about the way people were handling the situation. The media. The feds. The medical establishment. I guess being a food critic for the *Sun-Times* filled him with an intense desire to critique everything. Never mind the fact he was freaking out just as much as everyone else, including me, despite being five years younger.

I opened the door to find two men, neither of whom was my crotchety neighbor Ted. One was tall, the other about my height. They both wore cheap gray pants with a navy sweater and looked to be in their late twenties.

"Mr. Remis?" the tall one asked with a fake smile.

"Uh, yes," I replied, wondering who these two very serious-looking guys were. I instinctively shifted the door closed a thousandth of an inch, but the move didn't escape the taller man's attention.

"There's no need to worry," he said, handing over a business card. "Just here for a routine chat. May we come in?"

I checked the card and felt the blood drain from my face. The letters ETF were emblazoned on the piece of thick card stock in gold. Underneath, the man's name and title: Fred Langdon, Field Representative. I'd heard about these field representatives. Everyone had. They were the people who tracked down expiration hoppers. The title of representative had just enough ambiguity to it. What kind of powers of enforcement did they have? Looking at Langdon and his partner, my guess was absolute.

"Have I done something wrong?" I asked, stalling. To what end, I had no idea.

"Of course not, Mr. Remis," the shorter field rep chimed in. "Nothing that we know of anyway." He said the last part with a creepy chuckle that made me want to bolt for the door leading to the fire escape. But then again, what was I really worried about? It's not like they could read my thoughts. They had no idea I was planning to disappear in Idaho or wherever. Although they could have been following my internet habits. I knew I shouldn't have Googled all those driving routes!

Without any real options, and in the hopes of projecting a calm demeanor, I slid the door open and stepped aside. The reps walked in and headed toward the living room.

"Please, sit down," I said. "Something to drink?"

"No, no. This is our ninth visit already today. If I have another cup of coffee, I might just explode," said Langdon.

Ninth visit. Okay. Visit. What exactly did that mean? And why did he mention it was their ninth one of the day? Was he trying to intimidate me? As I pondered that, I realized the two men were sitting on the couch while I was standing in the middle of the room. I spun my computer chair around to face them, giving the screen a quick glance to see what window I'd left open—luckily it was just a medical research page and not Google Maps. I sat in the chair.

And waited.

Finally, Langdon spoke. "Are you familiar with the ETF?"

"Somewhat."

"I know the feeling," Langdon joked. "Jones and I have been doing this two weeks, and I'm still learning something new about the Expiration Task Force every day. Did you know we're a part of HHS and also, technically, Homeland Security?"

"I think I saw something online about that," I said. It was all over Reddit, actually.

"Don't believe everything you read online, I can tell you that," Langdon said, trying for a light tone but missing the mark. It came off as particularly defensive.

For the first time, I noticed his partner, Jones, had a black case of some kind with him. If I didn't know any better, I would have said it was a medical case.

"Regardless, we're just here to check in on you. As I'm sure you're quite aware, you're kinda getting up there in age!" he joked. "You look great, though. In fact, out of all the people we've seen today, I'd say you might be the most likely, based purely on appearances, to be the next Patient K."

I wasn't sure how to respond, so I didn't. Langdon proceeded.

"Now, if you've been visiting sites like, I don't know, Reddit, you probably know all about our most public and flashy role: locating forty-somethings. But that's really just a tiny fraction of what the ETF does. Jones and I don't even do that at all. Do we, Jones?"

His partner shook his head.

"See, Mr. Remis ... can I call you William? See, William, we actually talk to people like you as a public service. For the most part, we're like boring census takers. We have questions about your mood, health, things of that nature. Then we take all those answers and put them into a double-blind database to gauge how this ... well, I don't want to call it a crisis ... how this medical situation is affecting the nation. It will help inform policy."

"Completely painless," Jones added.

I was completely freaked out at this point. I could feel my heart racing, and my first thought was that these guys were killing me by wasting all those extra beats. Sensing my concern, Langdon produced a tablet with a survey screen on it.

"Harmless. Look, question one: How old are you?" he read. "I already know this one."

He typed in the answer. The questions that followed were of the standard variety, confirming my place of birth, occupation, family history, and general health background. While the whole conversation felt invasive and Big Brotherish, I had to admit the survey itself seemed fairly benign. And aside from being creepy, the two reps were just government officials doing their jobs. They appeared to take a passing interest in my years working in advertising. Jones asked if I had worked on any commercials he might remember. I lied and said no. I was pretty sure he'd know my work for Aurora Trucks, thanks to the famous ad I'd come up with that showed the vehicle driving on the moon with the tagline, "Go literally anywhere." It was a simple enough idea, but the commercial was shot by a hot director at the time, and he delivered the goods. I got some of the credit for the visuals, being the art director on it. It was one of those projects that earned just enough awards and fame to keep me comfortably employed for the next few years, even if I only came up with terrible ideas. Which I may or may not have. My early twenties were a bit blurry.

Langdon scanned the tablet and nodded. "That's all the questions we have. Except for the book."

I had a feeling that was coming.

"I haven't read it myself, but the note here calls it subversive," he said. "How do you feel about that?"

"The fact that you haven't read it? Or the subversive part?" I joked.

He just waited for an actual response.

"I'm not sure I'd label it subversive. I wrote it mostly on a lark. I guess I believed most of it at the time, but that was years ago," I explained. It was the truth. I don't think anyone truly believes what they did or thought when they were young. Life has a way of changing your mind on almost every subject.

"I'm asking specifically about the part where you claim that the one thing standing between a peaceful society and anarchy was the forty-year lifespan," he said, referencing a note on his tablet.

"Did I write that? I'm an old man, Mr. Langdon. Twenty years ago … I probably just thought it was a provocative thing to say. I also wrote that sex was better with total strangers, and I don't know if that was the smartest statement either."

He and Jones took a few moments to consider my response. Finally, Jones nodded to his partner.

"I don't think the old dude is going to be fomenting anarchy anytime soon," he said as if I wasn't even there. I was simultaneously pissed about the comment and surprised the word *fomenting* was part of his vocabulary.

"As you know, we are asking all people near expiration to refrain from traveling," Langdon said, changing the subject. "We understand the inconvenience, especially at a time when folks would like to be near their loved ones, which is why we're offering tax credits for family members who have to travel to see their loved ones before they expire."

"Yeah, I don't have any family, so ... won't be an issue for me."

"Perfect," said Jones, with no hint of irony in his voice. "Still, we've found that a not insignificant percentage of near-expireds are contemplating, for lack of a better term, hiding out. While it certainly sounds like you have no such plans, we do need to take a simple precaution."

He then reached into his medical bag and removed a small leather case. After unzipping it, he removed a silver tube with a valve trigger on the side.

"What the hell is that?"

"Relax, Bill, it's not a drug of any kind," Langdon said in his most assuring voice. "It's a tracking device. You won't even feel it. Slips right under the epidermis."

"What?"

"That's your skin, Bill," Jones deadpanned.

"I know what the fuck my epidermis is!" I shouted.

The two reps went a bit rigid, not taking kindly to my sudden change in demeanor.

"Is there a reason you don't want a tracking device on your person?" Langdon asked, leaning forward.

"I can think of a lot of them," I said. "In the first place, I'm pretty sure you don't have the right to do that."

Jones made a clicking sound with his teeth and shrugged. "It turns out, we kinda do. But you are free to refuse the device."

"Okay, I refuse."

He started putting the tube away.

That was easy, I thought.

"If you want to gather some of your belongings, we can take you to the detention facility directly," Langdon said. "It's a safe and comfortable place for you to spend your remaining days."

Chapter 5

They knew where I was at all times. The grocery store. McGee's. The bathroom. I doubt they were all sitting in a room somewhere monitoring how often I walked from my apartment to the grocery store, but they could if they wanted. That was unnerving.

Aside from a slight pinch when Jones popped the device into the fleshy part of my shoulder, the implant's lasting effects were all mental. I could *feel* it inside me. More importantly, it had blown up my plan to drive out of Chicago to a destination unknown. After doing some research online, I was convinced of an even greater concern: the chip wasn't just tracking my location, it was tracking my vitals. So, the second I lived a second too long, the ETF would know. Then they'd converge on my location and whisk me away to a facility that would undoubtedly be just as safe and comfortable as the one they offered me earlier.

That is, if I lived to be a forty-something. Only 184 people had made it past their expiration dates. The number was rising, to be sure, but my chances were still better of winning the lottery than being immortal. (The internet's word, not mine. I realize living an extra few days or months does not constitute immortality.)

I decided to move forward with my plan. All I had to do was find someone to cut out the tracker. The ETF was clever in their placement on the back of the shoulder. It meant removing the implant by myself was impossible. While I was sure the device had some alert it would send out when removed or destroyed, I figured if I was ready to bolt the moment the tracker was out, I should be good.

That removal process, though.

It had to be someone I trusted … and who trusted me. The list was painfully short. My first thought was Marisa, Paul's sister. She would probably do it, except for one problem: she was extremely squeamish around blood. One time when she, Paul and I had gone rock climbing, she nearly fainted when Paul gashed his leg open. Having to jam a knife into my shoulder to retrieve a small object might be too much for her, especially if she didn't get it on the first try. That left … um … my neighbor Ted? Given his distrust of the ETF, he'd probably be willing to help, if only out of spite. And I was reasonably sure he wouldn't say anything about it if (a) he didn't want to do it or (b) the field reps somehow discovered his involvement. Besides, he owed me for all the times I'd listened to his rants over the years.

I tried knocking on Ted's door a few times. No luck. Figuring he must have been at some hot new restaurant or taco stand in advance of a scathing review, I started to head back to my apartment. Our mutual neighbor Tricia stepped out into the hallway.

"You looking for Ted?" she asked.

Great. She must have heard me knocking. The last thing I needed was for Tricia to get even the faintest whiff of my plan. She loved to gossip.

"Yeah, was gonna see if he had any spare eggs. The store was out again," I lied.

"Oh, he won't need eggs where he's going."

"What are you talking about?"

Tricia sneered in delight, clearly excited about being able to pass along some juicy information. "Guess you didn't hear all the screaming and noise this afternoon either," she said, lighting a cigarette.

"I must have been at the store ..."

"Right, not getting those eggs. Funny thing. I was at the market this morning, and they were all stocked up. Anyway, Ted's mouth finally got him in trouble. Saw a couple ETF agents hauling him away right after lunch. He was screaming bloody murder!"

"What do you mean his mouth finally got him in trouble?" I asked.

"Well, his fingers, I guess. I wasn't trying to hear or nothing, but it's hard not to when the guy is screaming at the top of his lungs. He kept saying those posts on Reddit weren't from him ... but I mean, any fool could tell he was lying. I don't know which is worse, his reviews or his lying skills."

"Wow, I didn't even know he was posting on Reddit. Do you know what he was saying?"

Tricia shook her head and narrowed her eyes. "You're a little better at lying, but not by much. Say, aren't you getting close to expiration? They put one of those trackers in you yet?"

I didn't answer. I just grimaced and headed back toward my apartment to plop down onto the bed, shaken. It's one thing to hear rumors about the government abducting people in the middle of the night—or worse, broad daylight—but entirely another to have it happen to someone you know. Ted had spoken out. And now Ted was gone. Would he be back? And if so, when? I wouldn't exactly call him my best friend, but the guy didn't deserve to be dragged away just because of his miserable attitude and propensity to spout conspiracies online. Although they didn't much feel like conspiracies at the moment.

I turned my attention to the TV, where the news anchor was touting the latest numbers: 254 confirmed forty-somethings. The list was growing. It should be cause for celebration, but more and more it felt like my world was crashing in on me. I grabbed a bottle of vodka from the cabinet and took a healthy swig, then poured myself a glass. I needed to think. With Ted gone, who was going to remove that damn tracker? And why did I want it out so bad? I should probably be focusing more time on getting laid or settling my affairs instead of the pipe dream that I might be that one in a hundred million.

Wait a minute.

Laid.

That gave me an idea.

Chapter 6

The coffee shop was bustling with activity. I took a sip of my latte and mused at the name scrawled on the cup in black marker: Wilt. Was it really that hard to remember the name William or Will? How many Wilts were there in the world, anyhow? I bet none of them were living past expiration. It was a depressing thought. Entire names would be left out of the evolutionary lottery. I scanned the cups of other nearby customers. Sheila. Pretty rare. Doubt any Sheilas were going to be celebrating day 14,611 anytime soon. Same for you, Victar. Although that was probably Victor. The baristas did the misspellings on purpose. A grand joke that everybody was in on. Either way, Victor/Victar had about as much chance of living post-expiration as Joleen did.

I checked my watch. Dana was already fifteen minutes late. She had agreed to meet me on her lunch break, but I was beginning to think she might not show. We'd only spent a few hours together, and it seemed like a lifetime ago, so I couldn't exactly blame her. I found myself involuntarily scratching my shoulder again.

"Fleas?" Dana joked as she plopped down in the chair opposite me. "A little veterinary humor, sorry."

She looked different in her blue vet tech uniform and lack of makeup. Younger.

"Want me to order you a cup?" I offered.

"Thanks, but I have to get back in a bit," she said, balancing between being polite and not wanting to commit too much to the date. Or meetup. Or whatever she assumed this was. "You said it was important?"

"Yeah, first, thanks for coming. I know it's been crazy since we, you know ..."

"Hooked up?"

"Right. Which I enjoyed, by the way."

"I did too," she said with a hint of a smile. The moment passed quickly, however, and she looked at me and waited.

"So, vet tech. What's that like?"

Dana frowned a bit, then took pity on me. "Look, I really did have a good time the other night. But I'm not into relationships so much, especially ... I mean, no offense, but you're maybe a bit close to the end?"

I was. No denying it. A lot closer than she knew, too. She actually was about to continue, then held her tongue.

"What?" I asked.

"Nothing. It's nothing," she lied, then perked back up. "Tell me, Bill, what's the super-secret reason we had to meet today?"

My mouth went dry. I took another gulp of coffee and tried to game out the best way to broach the subject. In the end, I gave up and went the direct route. "I need your help. I don't have anyone else to ask."

"Okay ..." She nodded, motioning for me to spit it out.

"How much do you know about the ETF?"

"About the same as everyone else knows from the internet," she offered. "Wait, is it true? Are they really visiting people like you?"

"People like me?"

"I mean … I just heard …"

That nagging feeling I had when I first met her at McGee's was back and kicking into overdrive. I decided to level with her. "By people like me, you mean old people. Specifically, short-timers that are within sixty days of expiration."

She didn't deny it.

"How did you know my age?" I asked.

It was her turn to squirm. She sighed and looked me in the eyes. "I really did have a good time, you know."

"But …"

"But your friend Paul paid me to pick you up at that bar," she said.

I wasn't quite shocked by the news, but it definitely stung.

"It was his going-away present, he called it," she added, trying to lessen the impact. "I guess *I* was the present. I don't normally do this, though, and he totally said it was up to me if I wanted to go through with it. He wasn't paying me to have sex with you, per se."

"Per se," I repeated as I stood up. I was already a few steps from the table before she could respond.

She caught up with me on the street outside.

"Bill, wait," she pleaded. "C'mon, let me explain."

I stopped and turned. She paused and then shrugged. "Yeah, that was kinda the whole explanation," she admitted. "But you and I both had a good time. Isn't that what matters?"

I wasn't sure if I was more angry or ashamed. Paul obviously meant well, the bastard. It still felt embarrassing that Dana had played me for such a fool. Was I really that undesirable? I was. Marisa had taken pity on me. Dana had slept with me for payment. I guess I should have expected this at my age. I took a moment to collect myself, then nodded.

"I don't feel so bad asking you for a favor now," I said.

* * *

On the way home, I stopped at the cheapest expiration facility I could find. It was sandwiched between a convenience store and a dry-cleaners. The sign in the window said they offered full cremation and disposal services for $499. I figured half a grand was worth creating a money trail to throw the ETF off my scent. If they thought I had every intention of going out the normal way, maybe they'd be less likely to give me trouble before I tried to disappear off the grid.

"Welcome to The Cremation Haven. I hope you're having a fine end to your life," the young teen working the counter said. "How may I help you expire?"

I scanned the menu board on the wall, searching for the cheapest option.

"The number five," I said, referring to the plan that covered body removal and cremation, then disposal of the ashes. Simple. No frills.

"Would you like an urn with that?" the teen asked, trying to upsell. He looked to be about fourteen and had probably just finished high school, so I didn't blame him for trying to make extra commission. He continued his spiel. "I can also upgrade you to the Friends & Family Dispersal Package for just $99.99 more, so your ashes can be sent to the three recipients of your choice."

I wondered how many people actually came into an expiration facility next to a dry-cleaners and decided, yeah, okay, I want to spend a lot of money on my death after all.

"No thanks, just the basics," I said.

"It's your funeral!" he joked.

I humored him with a thin smile.

About five minutes later, I had filled out all the requisite forms and indicated where I planned to be when I expired. I paid in advance for obvious reasons and turned down the complimentary Last Mint he offered me before I left.

With my disposal plans settled, I moved onto the next phase of my scheme: slowly removing enough cash from my bank account so I didn't arouse suspicion with lump sums. Paying in cash was critical to moving around the country without leaving a trace, but I only had a little over a week to amass enough cash before I hit the road. I withdrew $500 from the ATM, trying to appear as calm and casual for the video cameras as possible.

Chapter 7

Dana had agreed to cut out the tracker. The fact that she did so out of guilt didn't bother me. We were still far from even in my book. With a competent medical professional on board to remove the ETF device, I turned my attention to planning for life on the proverbial lam.

I cleared my laptop's browser cache, then rebooted the operating system to hopefully erase any traces of research on potential destinations. But just in case that didn't work, before the wipe, I spent a good hour plugging East Coast cities into my search engine to make the ETF think I was heading toward New York or Boston, when in reality I had decided on the western half of the country. Using a prepaid cell phone, I conducted all my research on Wi-Fi at my favorite smoothie shop. It was a bit of a money waste, as I was too concerned with my sugar intake to finish more than a third of their smallest smoothie, but the senior discount was nice, and I wanted some normalcy as I gamed out my second act, so to speak.

I was looking for three things in a new home city and state: affordable rent, plenty of nature, and a high percentage of retirees. It would be easier to blend in if I was surrounded by other seniors. Also, communities with an older population tended to have better healthcare options. If I was going to live past forty, there was no doubt I'd need that. How I would get it without giving my real name was a problem for another day.

I was sitting in my usual booth at the Smoothie Prince, considering Arizona as a strong candidate, when I saw the latest sensational story on the news: a potential link had been found among nearly three-quarters of the forty-somethings. Everyone in the shop swiveled their heads to the TV, and the manager turned up the volume.

"According to the Global Health Service, despite representing various racial and ethnic ancestries, a common factor for just under 75 percent of the post-expiration individuals has been identified," the news anchor said. Aware of the gravity of the situation and selfishly milking it for all it was worth, he paused for dramatic effect, before reciting those fateful three words.

"Abnormally large nostrils," he said with a completely straight face.

I involuntarily snorted through my own goddamn nostrils. The other Smoothie Prince customers were just as baffled. Was this some kind of fucking joke? Apparently, it wasn't, because the anchor continued with his ridiculous report. The screen switched to photos of different shapes and types of nostrils. I could feel myself breathing through my nose now. Did I have big nostrils? I'd never considered that before. What if mine were average … or worse yet, small? I guess since only 75 percent of forty-somethings had abnormally large nostrils, did that mean the rest had small ones?

I noticed a woman nearby who was studying my face, gauging the size of the holes in my nose. A few other people did the same. To me. To each other. Then they looked at themselves using their phone cameras. This is what society had been reduced to: desperately gaping at our own noses, fearing the worst but hoping for a miracle.

A memory suddenly shot through me like a bolt of lightning. There I was, in the junior high gymnasium, nervously asking Cindy Wells to dance with me at the Winter Mixer.

"Ew, not a chance, big nose!" she screeched, before laughing with her friends.

At the time, it was gutting. I spent months worried that my face was somehow deformed. But now my heart sings! I definitely had a larger-than-average nose. I was sure of it. I didn't know if that meant my nostrils were also wider or longer than normal, but it was definitely leaning in the right direction. I leapt from the table, energized, and left the smoothie bar so quickly, I nearly smashed my aforementioned nose into the glass on my way out.

A few minutes later, I was back at my apartment building. I just made it into the elevator before the doors slid closed. One of the newer tenants, Alex, was the only other person in the elevator. Alex was a sixteen-year-old car salesman who had recently moved to the big city from downstate Illinois. He nodded respectfully.

"Mr. Remis," he said, smiling with deference.

"Hello, Alex," I said, still a bit winded after hurrying home from Smoothie Prince. "Feel free to call me Bill."

"Okay … Bill," he said, forcing it out. "Sorry, I was always taught to respect my elders. Say, are you okay?"

"I'm fine, why?"

"I just noticed you limping a bit when you were trying to make it to the elevator in time," he said. "I guess that comes with the territory!"

Had I been limping? I didn't even notice. That was par for

the course after age thirty-five. The little body aches and pains started adding up. One day you're fine, and the next day your skin is saggy and you've got a limp you don't even know about.

"Yeah, I hurt it playing basketball the other day," I lied, embarrassed about the state of my knees. He knew I was lying but let it go.

"How about those forty-somethings?" he asked, quickly changing the subject. "You could be next."

"Ha, maybe," I laughed, a bit too hard.

Alex also pushed out a chuckle.

Awkward.

The elevator stopped, and the doors opened with a ding.

"See you tomorrow," he said as he stepped into the hallway. "Unless I don't!"

As the doors closed, he stopped and quickly turned around. "I didn't mean cause, you know, I just say that all the time to people—"

The doors mercifully closed on his stupid face. He was a nice guy, but I wasn't in the mood to tolerate people who had decades left to flounder around and have fun. Youth truly is wasted on the young. Whatever. I had more important matters to deal with.

Chapter 8

Diameter. Circumference. I measured my nostrils five ways from Sunday. The first thing I learned was that my right nostril was two centimeters wider than the left one. Maybe that was a good thing.

After watching multiple newscasts and consulting a few websites using the browser on my prepaid phone, I was pretty sure Cindy Wells was right: I had, technically speaking, a large nose—and that included the nostrils. Finally. Some luck for ol' Bill! My spirits buoyed by this new discovery, I set to work finalizing my exit plan.

Arizona it would be. It checked off all the boxes, and maybe I'd even get to see the Cubs play some spring training games out there. The drive was roughly twenty-six hours, meaning two days on the road and plenty of time to clear my thoughts. When I was middle-aged, I enjoyed taking long road trips across the country. I hardly even turned on the radio, as I found the time alone in my car was therapeutic. That was fifteen years ago, but I hoped the experience still held. When I reached Arizona, I'd start with a week in Scottsdale, and if that wasn't to my liking, I'd try Tucson. Should neither of those prove to be viable destinations, the next stop was Las Vegas.

The biggest snag in my plan was cash. A few ATM with-drawals were fine, but I needed a chunk of cash, not just a couple thousand dollars. That meant parting with my most prized possession.

Alex was surprised to see me when he opened the door to his apartment.

"Hey, Mr. Remis. Uh, Bill," he awkwardly corrected. "I didn't realize you knew which apartment I lived in."

"Mailboxes."

"Ah, right. So what's up? You okay?"

"I'm not dying or anything. Not at this very moment."

"That's good. And hey, I'm sorry about the other day, what I said in the elevator."

"Don't mention it," I said, dismissing his concern. "But I do need your help with something."

Alex's apartment had the same general layout as mine, minus the second bedroom. That's where the similarities ended. He was a young professional, after all, and I was a retiree. While my couch was plush and comfortable, his was sleek and leather. I practically slid off the damn thing when I sat down on it. Mounted on the wall across from me was a curved screen that served as Alex's TV, gaming system, and computer all in one.

I was pretty sure he'd just been smoking pot before I arrived.

"Want one?" he said, offering me a hard seltzer from the fridge. "It doesn't have any caffeine."

I hated hard seltzer, but in the spirit of camaraderie, I took the thin silver-and-black can. Lightning Paw, it was called. As we sipped our disgusting, clear alcoholic beverages, I made my proposition. I was hoping that despite his job as a salesman, he wouldn't pick up on the lies that were mixed in with the truths in my story.

"So, you want me to buy your car for like a third of its value?" he asked, after I finished my pitch. "In cash?"

"Exactly."

"Because you want to hire an escort."

I nodded, feigning embarrassment. "At my age, it's not easy to enjoy romance. I want to experience that one last time. Without any money in savings, my car is my only real asset," I lied. "So, everybody wins. You get a deal on a great car. I get the cash. And the government doesn't have to know about the sale until after I'm gone."

"I don't think the ETF cares if people sell—"

"They do. I know three friends that have been questioned for making suspicious life changes near the end," I said. "All I want is to have a good time before the end, not spend my remaining days in a cell somewhere."

Alex looked at me, considering my offer. He shook his head.

"It must be hard dealing with these choices," he lamented. "I'll give you a little over half the value in cash. I'll also let you use the car until you expire."

When Alex dropped by the next day with $4,500 in cash for the car, I decided to throw an extra $500 in the check I planned to leave for him when I skipped town. That would cover the cash he gave me, plus extra for the trouble. He was a good guy. Besides, he would see the check in his mailbox before he even knew I was gone with the car. So really, no harm, no foul. He might even respect an old timer like me for putting one over on him.

Chapter 9

Dana lived on the west side in a part of Chicago known for rent control and frequent crime. The narrow streets were lined with vehicles, and it took about ten minutes to find a spot more than two blocks from her building. I felt a nervous twinge when I clicked the alarm and walked away from my car. The trunk and back seat were packed and ready to go, so if by chance someone happened to choose to steal my car in the half hour I was at Dana's, they would get all of my most important belongings.

I tapped her apartment number into the intercom and waited for the corresponding buzz of the doors, eyeing a suspicious teen who was walking down the street. Was he looking for a car to steal? No, I was being paranoid. The door buzz surprised me, and I felt a little urine squeak out. Or maybe I had imagined it—loss of bladder control was a sign of aging, of which I was acutely aware these days. I opened the door and entered the building, hoping to make this visit short and sweet, so I could get on the road and on to my great adventure.

Dana's apartment was small, even by this neighborhood's standards. Seeing her at home presented another version of her I never would have guessed: painter. The living room was her studio and was filled with artwork in various states of completion. Most of the finished pieces on the walls were idealistic landscapes, but her works in progress on and around the easel were a different tone entirely. More melancholy. They were portraits. I spent years in front of a computer creating layouts and digital artwork for ads, but this stuff was on a different level. I could see she had considerable skills, both natural and practiced, especially given the range of work in her apartment. The landscapes and portraits were equally impressive in their own ways. There was a familiarity to the pieces that intrigued me.

"I like your art," I said.

"Thanks," she replied, putting her hair into a ponytail as she led me down the hall to the kitchen. "Your friend did too."

That's when it dawned on me. Her art seemed familiar because Paul had been one of her customers. That must have been how they met. A few years ago, he had hung two landscapes in his bedroom; she'd painted them.

"Ah, I knew they looked familiar."

"What did he do with the pieces when he expired?" she asked.

"His sister took them. I don't know if she's really a collector, but they had sentimental value," I said. "I know Paul really liked them."

Dana motioned for me to sit down at the kitchen table. Her kit was already there and ready to go. Swabs. Alcohol. A syringe with what I assumed was local anesthetic. And a few scalpels. She saw me eyeing the instruments warily.

"You still want me to do this?"

"Yes."

"Okay then, take off your shirt."

I'd been nervous about this part. She had already seen me naked, but it was dark, we were drunk, and she'd been paid to refrain from (overtly) judging me. This time there was plenty of natural light, we were both sober, and I was just some old flabby dude who needed her help gouging a metal device out of my back. She noticed my hesitation and her eyes softened.

"You look good for your age, trust me," she said.

I pulled off my T-shirt and set it on my lap.

"Here's the plan," she explained, picking up the syringe. "First, I'm going to give you this shot, which should numb the area at least enough to where you won't pass out from the pain. Then I'm going to try fishing the sucker out. I can see the small scar where they put it in … but it goes without saying I have no idea what it looks like or exactly where it might have shifted."

"I understand. Just do your best."

"Also, you're not a golden retriever, so there's that nuance to consider."

I laughed. Nodded. I just wanted her to get on with it.

Without any warning, she jabbed me with the needle. I jumped a bit, startled, then looked over my shoulder at her.

"I figured it would be better to surprise you. No?"

"Not really."

"Good to know for the future," she joked.

After removing the needle, she plunked down in the chair opposite me. "Now we wait about five minutes. I think. I had to adjust the dose for your weight, so there's a chance I got it wrong. Just tell me when you start to feel your shoulder go numb."

We sat there for a few moments in awkward silence. She cleared her throat and was about to say something, when she stopped herself.

"What?"

"I wanted to apologize again. Paul thought it was a good idea, and I really did need the money."

"What for?"

"The money? Lawyer fees. I've been trying to get custody of my son ..."

For the first time, I noticed the art on the fridge. It wasn't hers. The drawings were good, but clearly made by someone much younger.

"How old is he?"

"Just turned nine."

"What are the chances you'll get custody?"

"I actually did last week," she said, with a smile in her eyes. "You wanna meet him?"

"Uh ... maybe after I have my shirt back on?" I replied. "Is he here?"

"Relax, he's playing video games in his bedroom. We could shout at the top of our lungs, and all he'd hear is the explosions in his headphones."

"I think I'm starting to feel the anesthetic," I said, rubbing my shoulder.

"His name's Hank, and he's a great kid," she added as she fidgeted with her rubber gloves. She picked up the scalpel, then paused.

"It's okay," I assured her. "I don't expect it to be perfect. And I think I have a decent tolerance for pain."

"The thing is, it's not that," she said, putting the scalpel back down. "I'm gonna need a favor from you in return for me doing this."

It turned out Dana wanted me to drive her and her son wherever I was headed, as long as it was away from Chicago and her ex-husband, who apparently didn't take the custody ruling well. Dana feared not only for her son but also her own safety.

I don't know what I expected her to ask of me, but it wasn't that.

As she explained the situation, I noticed a pair of suitcases sitting in the hallway just off the kitchen. They were ready to go. Immediately. I wasn't sure exactly how to respond. My first instinct was to say I would do it so that she'd go forward with removing the tracker. Once it was gone, I could just refuse to take her. Ethical? No. Practical? Very much so. I mean, I had gone to a lot of trouble to plan my escape; having her and her son along would present a host of problems. Was she going to use her credit card? If so, she was trackable. For all I knew, her ex was the kind of guy who would have her followed to the ends of the earth. Also, I barely knew this woman. Having her tag along for a couple days was not the best idea.

Of course, that was simply my first instinct. Most people rarely have the luxury of following those. Many of us refuse to admit it, but we are all extremely selfish at heart. If we let that selfishness guide us, unchecked, the world would be a pretty terrible place. Most of us don't act on those base instincts, however. We usually take time to let our morals and ethics get involved.

In this case, she wanted a way out. And she needed my help. Just like I needed hers.

"I can drop you off in Colorado or New Mexico," I said. "I can't take you to my destination because it wouldn't be safe for me—or you—if you knew where that was."

"Deal," she replied with a sigh of relief. Then she handed me a wooden spoon. "Now bite down on this."

* * *

Hank had his mother's eyes. He was a shy kid with a certain sadness about him. I pushed aside a small box of books so he could load his suitcase into the back seat. Hank was hemmed in on both sides, stuck between my boxes and his luggage. He seemed fine with it.

"Thanks for the ride," he said to me, before looking at his mom, who undoubtedly had told him to be respectful and on his best behavior. Then he popped his headphones on and went back to the video game on his mobile.

I looked over at Dana in the passenger seat. "Does he know you're leaving for good?"

"It was his idea," Dana said. "Are you sure your shoulder is okay to drive?"

The sharp, searing pain had already begun to dissipate, replaced by a gnawing ache that would probably be there for a day or two. All in all, it wasn't so bad. I was glad to be free of the thing—and the ETF with it. I checked my mirrors yet again, assuming a full extraction team would come screeching around the corner any minute. Instead, there was no one.

Dana had removed the device like a pro. From first cut to last stitch, it might have taken a total of fifteen minutes. I wondered whether maybe she had a background in general medical treatment before somehow ending up as a vet tech. She definitely had the skill and coordination to entertain the surgeon path. At least that was my take after going under the knife in her kitchen, so maybe my perspective was skewed. Regardless, I was glad I ended up going with her and not Ted.

"I'll be all right, Doc," I said with a smile. "Next stop ... somewhere in Missouri for lunch."

Chapter 10

Five more days.

According to all of recorded human history up until a few weeks ago, I had five days left to live. While I harbored an irrational belief that I was somehow destined to live into my forties, I had also built a contingency plan for enjoying days 14,605 to 14,610. You know, just in case. I didn't need to go out on a bender like Paul, but I didn't want to live my last week like a monk either.

So, I ordered the double cheeseburger and a large chocolate shake. Fuck it.

We'd driven straight from Chicago into Missouri and had decided to stop for lunch about a half hour west of St. Louis. It was a diner called Joe's with a real small-town feel. It reminded me of my youth, growing up in downstate Illinois. Dana and I engaged in a little awkward chit-chat at the beginning of the ride but eventually settled for the radio. It wasn't what I'd hoped for when I was thinking of a solitary ride west. Still, it wasn't altogether unpleasant. Hank was focused on his game, and Dana did her best to blend into the background in an effort to minimize the intrusion.

Sitting at the diner, however, required conversation. You can go hours without speaking in a car, but eating a meal in silence is unnerving.

"What game is he playing?" I asked Dana, referring to the game Hank had been glued to nearly the entire five hours I'd known him.

Dana took the device from Hank, prompting him to remove his headphones, upset. "Mr. Remis asked you a question," she said.

"You can call me Bill," I told him. "I was just asking what game that is."

"Collateral Damage 8," he replied.

"I think I played 2 or 3 before," I said.

"They started at 6," he said, unimpressed.

Dana suppressed a laugh.

"Maybe it was another game," I offered, trying to recover.

"What system?"

"What?"

"You said it might have been a different game, so I was just wondering what system. I might know it. Bill."

I nodded. The kid was now fucking with me. Whatever happened to respecting your elders? I thought back to Alex's apartment and the pause screen on his TV when I dropped by. J-Box? M-Box? No ...

"X-Box," I declared, mostly confident.

Hank was dubious. "Could've been Acts of War, I guess."

"Oh look, the food!" I practically shouted, hoping for a quick change of subject.

The waiter, who wasn't much older than Hank, delivered our greasy burgers and fries, saving our milkshakes for last. It looked to be quite the feast.

"Can I listen to music while I eat?" Hank asked Dana.

She reluctantly gave her blessing, and he popped the headphones back on as he dug into his fries. Dana turned to me with a wise smile.

"I think I played 2 or 3," she mocked.

"I was trying to make conversation."

"First rule of talking to kids: don't lie. They always know."

"I'll keep that in mind for the rest of the trip. Nothing but truth from now on."

"Does that apply to me too?" she asked. When I didn't answer right away, she raised an eyebrow. "Do you really think you're going to live past expiration?"

I took a slow sip of my chocolate milkshake and made her wait for my response. If I was taking her advice and being honest with kids, her, and myself, I would've said no. Deep down I knew it was ridiculous. But so was dying at exactly the same time as everyone else. There was just nothing special about it. If anything, it was dehumanizing. The idea that everybody on the planet was programmed to live the same amount of time, with no deviation whatsoever, stripped any uniqueness from existing. And what makes us unique is what makes us human. So no, I refused to accept that, even though I knew I probably had no choice.

"Someone has to," I said.

Dana frowned at that but didn't pursue the line of questioning further. I decided to turn the tables.

"Do you really think you can disappear from your ex? All he has to do is get your credit card or bank records to see where you've been spending money."

"True. But he'd be looking for the wrong person," Dana said. She slid her ID across the table. It had a current pic of her with the name Diane Fawcey. It was an Idaho license.

"This must have been expensive," I noted, admiring the quality.

"The other thing Paul's money helped pay for," she said. "Shit, I didn't mean it like that."

"Sure you did. It's okay. I'm glad the money went to good use," I replied. And I actually meant it. I was also more focused on the license. I'd thought about giving myself a new identity but had no connections to the world of fake IDs and the like. Now, that seemed promising. "Think your person could make one for me?"

"Ask him when he's done with his lunch," she said, motioning to Hank. "This kid is scary with the Internet and the right materials. He just made the ID, though. If you want the whole social security number and all that, it'll cost about a thousand dollars, and I could probably put you in touch."

I did some quick math in my head, trying to figure out how much Paul had paid her to sleep with me. I needed to stop focusing on that. The truth is I wanted to believe Dana when she said she had a good time—I'd felt a connection with her that night. Not that it mattered now. In about twenty-four hours, we'd be heading our separate ways to new lives.

Out of the corner of my eye, I saw two flashes of gray. I turned to find two field reps wearing the same navy sweaters and gray pants as Langdon and Jones. My heart began to race as they walked toward our table. How had they found me so quickly? I'd avoided tollways and their accompanying cameras and hadn't even brought my credit card with me just in case I was tempted to buy gas with it.

One of the field reps locked eyes with me … just before the two men turned and sat down a few booths away. I let out a sigh of relief.

"Paranoid much?" Dana asked.

"Ha, maybe a little."

"There are a few million people your age in the country. I doubt they're worried about you just yet. The odds ..."

Right. The odds. They probably weren't worried about me because the odds of me becoming a forty-something were so slim. To drive the point home, the waiter arrived with the check and asked if I was going to use a senior discount for the meal.

I was.

Chapter 11

Kansas is flat.

The two-lane highway was lined with brown fields on either side, and the road ahead seemed to stretch on forever. We saw another vehicle once every few minutes, tops. Dana and I couldn't take the music on the radio (mostly country blues, of which we weren't fans), so we turned on a news station. The official global count was up to 1,043 people who had crossed the Rubicon. On the one hand, it was nice to hear more people were outliving their expiration date. On the other, the percentage of the total population was still absurdly low.

That wasn't the biggest news, however.

Just an hour earlier, the NIH had announced a bombshell discovery linking nearly all the forty-somethings. Unlike abnormally large nostrils, which was tantalizing but offered no discernible underlying health rationale, this new link was more concrete: a missing genetic marker. The news report featured a clip of a geneticist trying to explain the way the marker worked, but he lost me after the second sentence. He apparently wasn't making sense to the reporter either, who thanked him and tried to paraphrase the monologue by saying, "What we know is that among all those post-expiration individuals tested, a specific aspect of their DNA that should be there ... simply wasn't."

"What the fuck does that even mean?" I asked, forgetting Hank was in the back seat. I checked the mirror and saw that he was still engrossed in his game, headphones and all.

"Aliens," Dana joked.

"How could somebody be missing part of their DNA?" I wondered aloud. "And how are all those people living longer?"

Dana shook her head. No idea.

I was at t-minus five days here. I needed answers. The news report continued, mostly rehashing the same information, which made sense, as nobody could divine the implications of such a discovery, not even the doctors who made it. Apparently, they'd never even heard of a person missing this particular marker, let alone an entire group of people having the same condition.

I was so lost in thought, I nearly rammed into the car in front of us on the highway as we suddenly arrived at a bottleneck. Weird. The highway had been practically desolate ten minutes earlier.

"First, people living over forty. Now a traffic jam in the middle of Kansas. I've seen it all," said Dana.

As we rolled to a stop, I opened my window and leaned my head out to get a look at what was causing the backup. I didn't see any ambulances or fire trucks, suggesting the most likely issue, an accident, wasn't the problem. I felt a knot in the pit of my stomach when I saw, about fifty cars ahead, orange cones flanked by a pair of state police cruisers.

"Fuck," I muttered.

"What is it?"

"Some kind of checkpoint."

Dana could see what I was thinking. "I doubt it's for you. It's probably a sobriety check."

"I don't think it's for me, *personally*," I said. "But it could be for people my age, trying to make sure we're not moving about."

"A random roadblock on a highway ... looking for what? Old people?"

I exhaled and tried to relax. I was not in the right frame of mind. Sobriety checkpoint was the obvious answer here, especially given how frazzled some people were about the news. The authorities still had to keep the roads safe, even if society was on the brink of changing forever. I remained a bit on edge, however, until about twenty minutes later, when I saw one of the officers holding a Breathalyzer. Finally at ease, I focused back on the news about the genetic marker.

Of all the hot takes we'd heard on the radio in the past twenty minutes, one stood out to me as the most plausible. A geneticist explained that many single-gene disorders such as Tay-Sachs and sickle-cell anemia were hereditary. One likely explanation for a widespread gene disorder such as a missing genetic marker was a common ancestor. Even seemingly unrelated people from around the globe could be descendants of the same individual or group of individuals twenty to thirty generations earlier. If that was the case, the geneticist reasoned, we could be looking at a very specific gene mutation that took a very specific number of years to fully manifest. It made sense.

"That makes no sense," Dana disagreed.

"I kinda thought it was on the mark."

"No way," she said, confident. "Let's say it was twenty generations earlier. Yes, we know all the descendants since then had the same max age. Forty years. But in all those different branches, there were probably some people who died early, had kids early, had kids late, whatever. The idea that suddenly every branch of the tree is now coming to fruition at the same time with this mutation … it's dumber than the alien theory. I actually think the alien dude might be right!"

"The guy from Romania who said the forty-somethings are all descended from aliens?"

"Who cares if he's from Romania? And he said they were all descended from aliens *or* had been modified by aliens."

"Oh, I'm sorry for not including that. So, they were all abducted and then had their genetics changed to let them live longer."

"Makes more sense than some superstud spreading his seed six hundred years ago."

It was a fair point.

* * *

I rolled my window down and smiled at the veteran patrolman. He looked to be in his mid-thirties. "Afternoon, officer."

"Hi there," he said, glancing at Dana in the passenger seat and then Hank in the back, squeezed between all my belongings. "Packed in there. Where you headed?"

"Arizona, eventually," I replied, not wanting to give any more information than was necessary.

"Spent a few years in Phoenix. Nice city," said the officer. "We're just doing a sobriety check. Would you object to a field Breathalyzer test? You can refuse if you'd rather go to the station."

"Not at all. I'd be happy to take the test. I appreciate you guys keeping the roads safe," I said. I was laying it on a bit thick, but better to be safe than sorry.

"If I can get your license, we'll try to make this quick," he said.

I hadn't thought about that. Technically, I wasn't supposed to be crossing state lines. I traded a worried glance with Dana as I removed my ID from my wallet and handed it over.

The officer scanned it with a handheld device and waited for the information and status to appear on the screen.

Was it possible they already had me flagged in the national database? I could feel the cut on my shoulder pulsing against the bandage as tiny beads of sweat formed on my brow. The officer's handheld buzzed. He looked at the screen, then handed me back my license.

"Pretty close to expiration," he said, looking over the car with interest. "Getting your affairs in order?"

I froze and was just about to jam my foot on the gas in panic when Dana piped up.

"He's helping me and my son move to Arizona, then driving back in time for his funeral. I wanted to go, but I have a new job I'm starting on Monday," she lied. Hopefully, the cop didn't look too closely at the items packed in the back seat—or the trunk—as they were all clearly things that made more sense in my possession than hers.

"And they say chivalry is dead," the officer joked. Then he waved off his colleague who was approaching with the Breathalyzer. "I think we can trust this old-timer here," he told the younger officer.

"Thanks," I said, trying to conceal my extreme relief. I nearly dropped my license as I put it back in my wallet. As we pulled through the checkpoint, I caught Dana throwing me a wry smile.

"You owe me again," she joked.

Chapter 12

I had two days left to live. Maybe.

As I parked the car outside a motel in the outskirts of Denver, the moment had a bittersweet feel to it. Dana and Hank were going to start their new life here, while I would be pushing on to Arizona. I was going to miss Dana. Given my age and her situation, I didn't have any illusions about a romantic relationship with her. But we definitely got along well. There was a lack of awkwardness about our dynamic, something I hadn't experienced in decades with another woman. It wasn't exactly like hanging out with Paul, but it wasn't far off. We clicked. I think that's how non-seniors explained it.

Once I finished helping her and Hank gather their stuff from the car, I waited with Dana's son as she secured a room.

"Thanks, Mr. Remis," Hank said.

"No problem."

"You think my dad will be able to find us here?"

It was the first time he'd mentioned his father the entire trip. I took a look at the mountains and realized why Dana had chosen Colorado. Her art. The landscapes I saw in her apartment would be no match for what she'd create with inspiration like this all around. It was a risk going to such a picturesque setting;

it was the kind of location a smart private eye might hone in on if his client was smart enough to realize she might move somewhere with scenic surroundings. Her ex didn't seem that insightful, based on the little she'd spoken of him. I turned my gaze back on the sandy-haired boy, with his giant headphones and mature eyes.

"Your mom's too clever for that," I replied. "I think you are too. If you guys want to stay hidden, I have a feeling you will."

The boy nodded in agreement. Then he put his headphones back on as his mom exited the motel office and walked our way, holding the key card to their room.

"I guess this is it," she said, stopping a few feet from me. Then she turned to Hank and loudly asked him if he'd thanked me for the ride.

"Yup," Hank said without looking up from his screen.

Dana leaned in and gave me a kiss on the cheek. "You sure you don't want to stick around here for a couple days, in case things don't go your way? You know, just to have someone there at the end?"

It was a nice offer. Genuine. She didn't mean to make me sound pathetic by any means, but the idea of needing pity company at the end flew in the face of this whole endeavor. I wanted to live. If that wasn't in the cards, I wanted to die on my own terms.

"I think I should probably go," I said.

"You have my number if you change your mind. We'll be here a few days until I find some work," Dana said. "Arizona?"

I smiled. She'd guessed right, but I didn't want to give her the satisfaction.

"Fine, be that way," she said. "So long, Bill. For what it's worth, I did actually like your book. I read it back when it made the rounds, not that I was a groupie or anything."

* * *

The sun was beginning to set. It would take about thirteen hours to get to Scottsdale from Denver, so I planned to drive until midnight, then find a room for the night before the last stretch. With the radio off and nobody to engage in conversation, I could finally think.

The first thing that popped into my head was little green men. Aliens.

I couldn't shake the notion that this whole gene thing was engineered by forces beyond our control. What other explanation made sense? Evolution? No. A bunch of people across the globe did not suddenly start to evolve at the exact same time. I also didn't think any environmental triggers were at play, given the widespread nature of the phenomenon.

Assuming this wasn't a God thing, that left some kind of bioengineering experiment by Martians. Okay, they didn't have to be Martians. The point remains. Someone did this to us. They either did it many years ago and just decided to undo it recently or they somehow did it a few weeks ago. I was leaning toward the generations-ago theory.

I was also slamming on the brakes.

But it was too late.

I'd been so deep in thought, I hadn't seen the stalled eighteen-wheeler jackknifed up ahead. I tried to steer into the skid and regain control of the vehicle. I saw the undercarriage of the truck just before the world went black.

Chapter 13

The ceiling tiles had yellow discolorations at the edges. Humidity damage, probably, coupled with years of neglect. As I stared at them, I realized I didn't know why I was lying horizontal, trying to surmise the reason for the poor state of the ceiling above me.

"Hello, Mr. Remis," a man said. I looked to my right and saw a doctor standing at my bedside. Late twenties. Thick glasses. A plastic smile on his face. "How are you feeling?"

I didn't answer. I glanced around the room and tried to get my wits about me. Hospital. I was in a hospital. Judging by the ceiling and doofus-looking doctor, not a great one, either. I had tubes sticking out of my nose, wrist, and penis. I could feel my fingers and toes, so that was good.

"Mr. Remis?"

I'd get to him when I could, I decided. I continued trying to piece together my situation. I was alive and didn't seem to be paralyzed, which was nice. I did have a pretty severe headache, along with a pain in my right shoulder that pulsed all the way down my arm and into my hand. That constant beeping was going to get annoying. I guess Dr. Doofus noticed me eyeing the heart monitor next to the bed, because he turned down the volume. That was a good start.

"I ... where am I?" I managed.

"You're at St. David's Hospital in Durango, Colorado. You were in a car accident a few days ago. My name is Dr. Elgin."

A couple slices of memory came rushing back.

"That truck ..." I said, beginning to remember.

"It did cause quite a pileup," Dr. Elgin said. "Fortunately, you weren't more seriously injured. A few of the other people involved weren't so lucky."

"Oh." I wasn't sure how to respond to that. I definitely didn't feel lucky. Then something registered in my mind. Maybe it was the mix of drugs I was likely on, but it was taking me longer than usual to process information. "Days. What do you mean, days?"

A hint of a smile flickered across Elgin's face. He tried to suppress it and keep his professional demeanor, but I caught the flash of happiness. No, it was more smug than that. It was pride.

"Three days, in fact," he said, before leaning in. "So, I guess that means congratulations are in order. For both of us, in a way."

Three days. No doubt he'd pulled my records and was congratulating me on the fact that I was 14,612 days old.

I was forty-something.

It was not supposed to be this way. The elation I should have felt about passing my expiration date was extinguished by the fact I was in a hospital and not celebrating by myself at some remote location where nobody could find and dissect me.

I mean, fuck. It was awesome! And a disaster at the same time. I didn't want to end up in some lab being probed and prodded for the rest of my extended life. Oh no ... what if I was already there? What if this *was* the lab?

No.

Dr. Doofus wouldn't be in charge of something like that. Which means I might still have time to escape before the ETF arrived. I tried to push myself up from the bed, but I was too weak, my shoulder burned with searing pain, and my left hand wouldn't move.

I was cuffed to the bed.

"Relax, you're not going anywhere," the doctor said. "Not in that condition."

"Please excuse us, Dr. Elgin," a familiar voice said.

I looked to the door and saw Field Rep Langdon smiling back at me. He waited for the doctor to exit the room before he spoke again.

"You cost me lunch," he said. "Jones thought for sure you were a flight risk, but I pegged you for a stay-at-homer. We bet a sandwich at Mike's Diner on Broadway. Ever been there? It's good. A little pricey, but good."

"I'll keep that in mind." I had a gnawing in the pit of my stomach just looking at Langdon. I wasn't really in the mood to discuss food.

"I also thought you'd be happier when you woke up. After all, you dodged death twice," he said.

"Is this really necessary?" I asked, referring to the handcuff on my wrist.

Langdon raised an eyebrow, not even bothering to answer. He had to know about the missing tracker by now, as well as my obvious attempt to flee.

"What I can't figure out is, how did you know?" he mused.

"Know what?"

"That you were going to live past expiration."

I raised an eyebrow back at him. Better to say nothing and have him think I knew all along, rather than admit I was just blindly hoping for the best. Langdon sat in the chair next to the bed and sighed, pretending to commiserate with me.

"Bill, Bill, Bill," he said. "What are we going to do with you?"

"That's what I'd like to know."

"Last time we talked, I mentioned the greater good. Now's your chance, as forty-something number 1,408, to help other people. Don't you want to help people, Bill?"

One thousand four hundred eight. An exclusive club, all things considered. And too small for little old me to slip quietly into the night. Luckily, it was enough that I probably wouldn't be famous. After the first few hundred people, the media stopped delving into each individual's backstory and instead focused on connections and patterns in the survivor pool.

I felt the metal handcuff jangle on my hand as I weighed how to respond to Langdon. I wasn't sure it would matter anyway, as being a lab rat seemed compulsory at the moment. I wished I could punch that smug look off his face; clearly, I wanted to help people. But being forced to do so by the likes of him wasn't what I had in mind.

"Being assigned a number isn't the most reassuring development, if I'm being honest," I said.

"Ah, my coffee!" Langdon exclaimed, ignoring me. Jones had appeared in the doorway holding a pair of cups. He nodded hello. I didn't return the gesture. Langdon rose from the chair and headed to the door. Before exiting, he took a sip of his coffee and turned back to face me.

"If I'm being honest, your actions have made it pretty irrelevant what you think at this point," he said, all manner of pretense gone. "The doc says you'll be ready for transport in the morning.

69

The US government values you and what you have to offer, Bill. Despite what you might think of myself and Jones, we're not monsters. And you're not going to be shuttled away to some secret location. Just a facility where we are testing—and caring for—the post-expirees. Have a good night's sleep. There will be an officer outside should you need anything."

Or should I try to escape, he didn't say.

They had taken my cellphone and removed the landline. I was cut off from the outside world, aside from the TV that played classic sitcoms on rotation. While I was used to having my rights infringed upon as a result of my age, this felt more direct. Simply by not dying, I had become property of the state. Maybe they'd treat me like a hero wherever they took me in the morning, or maybe they'd carve me up and examine my parts.

Escape was going to be impossible, unfortunately. In addition to Dr. Doofus checking on me every hour, there was a uniformed police officer sitting right outside my door. The handcuffs also presented an obstacle. But if I somehow managed to overcome those three hurdles, I was home free, assuming I could secure a bus ticket without any ID or money.

Ah, the life of a forty-something!

Chapter 14

A fire alarm jarred me awake. The room had an orange hue to it, and my first thought was that the hospital was ablaze. Turns out it was just the first hints of the morning sun coming through the window.

The door burst open.

A nurse hurried in and started unplugging my equipment from the wall.

"Is there a fire?" I asked, still bleary-eyed from sleep.

"Yep, only thing I could think of," the nurse said. I took a closer look and realized the nurse was Dana. Someone yelled in the hall, causing Dana to freeze in panic. When the person ran past the open door and kept going, Dana continued unhooking my bed.

"You started the fire?"

"Surprise!" she joked, still focused on what she was doing.

"How are you even here?" I asked.

"I'll explain later." Dana removed a hairpin from her blonde locks. She'd dyed her hair.

"Are you seriously trying to ..." Before I could finish, she had popped the cuff of my wrist. "How did you do that?"

"Explaining time is later. Keep up. Now pull your catheter

out before I do."

I did as I was told. If this jailbreak was going to be successful, it was going to mean following her plan, whatever plan that was. I was just confused and along for the ride.

Damn, that catheter hurt to remove. No sooner had I discarded it than Dana was helping me up and then pushing me onto a gurney she'd brought into the room with her. I groaned in pain, gritting my teeth as a buzzsaw of heat cut through an entire side of my body.

"There, that wasn't so bad," Dana said with a smile. "Try to keep your head on the pillow and not look so ... freaked out. Although I guess a fire would scare most patients."

"I appreciate you trying to help me, but are you sure setting fire to a hospital was the best approach?"

"I never said it was the best approach. I just said it was the only thing I could think of," she replied.

As she pushed me through the doorway into the hall, I saw the empty chair where the cop had been sitting, watching over my room like a hawk. *He was probably helping with the fire. Smart.*

A couple of other patients were being moved on gurneys as well, creating chaos in the narrow corridor. I noticed the other nurses were all wearing light-green scrubs, while Dana's were blue; they were her old veterinary scrubs. This really was a rush job. Not that I was complaining. I mean, maybe she could have been gentler moving me out of my bed, but other than that, this seemed to be going well.

We made it to the elevator, but it was not in use. Fire. Right. Unfazed, Dana kept pushing me down the hall. Maybe there was an emergency elevator that ran during power outages and fire alarms? Nope. We got to the stairwell.

"Here comes the fun part," Dana said, reaching under the

gurney bed to retrieve a crutch. I grimaced just looking at it.

"You want to spend your extra time being a lab rat or sipping a beer poolside?" she asked rhetorically. She handed me the crutch and helped me onto my feet. "Congrats on your birthday, by the way. Kinda insane."

"As insane as this escape attempt?" I wondered aloud.

"No, probably not."

As I put weight on my good leg, my whole body cried out. Shoulder. Arm. Spleen. Or maybe kidneys. Who knew what was hurting, especially at this age? I considered making that joke to her, but there was no time, and I was conserving all my breath for wheezing through the throbbing pain in my shoulder. I had a bit of a panic attack when I realized I had no idea what floor we were on. Could have been the tenth for all I knew—the only view outside the window in my room from the POV of my bed was sky. I exhaled a sigh of relief when I saw the number four emblazoned on the door. Small victories, I told myself.

For the next few minutes, Dana used all her strength to help me down the flights of stairs to the main floor. Along the way, we were joined (and passed) by another nurse and patient, and then a friendly janitor helped me down the final two flights.

When we got to ground level, the janitor made his way into the main lobby of the hospital. Dana and I hung back. She peeked out the door and breathed deeply. "Two guards at the exit," she said. "Along with some serious assholes in navy sweaters."

"Those would be my assholes," I managed, still winded and wincing from the hobble down the stairs. "ETF."

Dana looked me up and down. "Think you can make it to the exit by yourself?"

"No, but I can try. What are you going to do?"

"Create a diversion."

"Not another fire, I hope."

"No, I have a better idea."

"Look, I don't know how to thank you for this," I said. It was true. I still didn't understand why she was going through all the trouble.

"Just find Hank outside in the lot. He'll be waiting in a white minivan."

"Jesus, Hank is here?"

"Who do you think set the fires while I rescued you?"

"Wait, did you say *fires*, plural?"

Dana didn't bother answering. She just sneaked out the door and headed right for Langdon and Jones. I watched through the cracked door as she told them something, then led them away from the exit area. The two guards were still there, but upon closer inspection, I realized they were ushering people through the checkpoint and outside, as the firefighters rushed in. That was my chance. I began my painful journey, using every ounce of my willpower to propel me forward. I tried to give off the appearance of someone in minimal pain, which was not easy.

When I got close to the guards, I did my best to turn my grimace into a smile. "Gentlemen," I said, "I was told we're supposed to head outside."

They gave me a long look, during which my heart nearly leapt out of my chest. Being a forty-something didn't make me immune to having a heart attack, I found myself musing.

"Actually, they say the fires have been contained," one of the guards said, after listening to his walkie. "You can wait in here until someone can get a wheelchair to bring you upstairs."

Fuck. What now? I spotted something in the pocket of the other guard.

"Actually, all this excitement has given me the jitters," I said. "I was hoping to duck outside for a quick smoke."

* * *

I was tempted to light up once I felt the cool morning breeze on my face. *Maybe later*, I thought. I slipped the cigarette I'd bummed off the guard into my pocket and hobbled my way through the dwindling crowd of patients and doctors in the hospital's parking lot. I didn't see a white minivan anywhere. *Damnit. Where's the kid?*

As I reached the roundabout, I heard tires squealing to a stop and turned just in time to see Hank behind the wheel of the vehicle. He had his headphones on. The automatic door slid open, and he nodded for me to get inside. Nothing like a nine-year-old getaway driver to cap off this escape. I barely had time to climb in before I heard a commotion behind me. It was Dana pushing through the crowd. She ran the last fifteen feet and dove into the still-open door.

"Go!" she yelled.

The minivan lurched ahead, and she nearly fell right back out of the vehicle—but I grabbed her arm just in time. She rolled all the way in and slammed the door behind her, then looked through the rear window. Langdon and Jones ran into the roundabout, their eyes locked on us. I didn't know whether to smile or duck, so I just collapsed in a heap onto the seat. Everything hurt. I was too tired to care if they jumped in a car to give chase. I closed my eyes and tried to let my muscles relax after the last ten minutes, which felt like hours.

I could hear Dana telling Hank where to turn and which streetlights to ignore. Eventually, she switched spots with him, and he plunked down on the seat behind me. I drifted in and out of sleep for the rest of the ride.

Chapter 15

In what was becoming a concerning trend, I once again woke up with no idea where I was.

After a few moments, I realized I was still in the minivan.

"We didn't want to disturb you," Dana said. She was leaning in the open door of the vehicle, a cup of coffee in her hand. She'd changed from her scrubs and was wearing a flannel shirt with jeans. They looked good on her. "We made it," she boasted with pride.

As if to punctuate the ridiculousness of that fact, a pig snorted. The minivan was parked in a barn. It was midday, judging by the sunlight streaking through the lone window of the old wooden structure. The snorts were soon followed by a few clucks. Pigs and chickens. I could kiss them all. I could also eat them all, I was so hungry.

I had three or four seconds of pure joy before the pain reintroduced itself in, oh, every part of my body. I felt old as hell. Which, yeah, I was. I was! I was older than almost everyone else in human history!

"Hungry?" Hank asked, arriving with cereal. I snatched the bowl from his hands and began to devour it like a wild animal. *Sorry, kid.* Over breakfast, I peppered Dana with questions about how they managed to break me out of the hospital. It started with a call she received a few days earlier from the medical staff; her number was the only one saved in my disposable cellphone. That was before I had turned forty.

Not wanting me to expire alone in a hospital, Dana decided to try to make it to Denver before my time was up. They were delayed a few hours after their first rental car stalled, however. Realizing they wouldn't get to the hospital in time, Dana called to confirm I had expired. She couldn't get a straight answer from the doctor and was eventually put in touch with Langdon, who was more concerned with learning about her than he was sharing any information about me.

"So, you just assumed I was alive?" I asked.

"It seemed crazy, but why else would they not tell me? I had to at least see for myself. I felt I owed you that much."

"Thank you," I said.

"Hey, don't thank me. It was Hank's idea to bust you out."

I looked over at the kid, who was predictably engrossed in his video game. According to Dana, when they arrived at the hospital, she sent Hank in to snoop around. He just kept going to different floors and asking for different room numbers until he finally wandered past the one I was in.

"At first I really couldn't believe you were alive. When Hank told me they had a cop outside your door, I got pissed. They had no right to hold you like that. I guess Hank could see how upset I was, so he just said we should get you out of there."

"And the fire?" I asked.

"Fires, multiple," she corrected.

"Yes. Fires. Multiple."

"We set a few controlled fires in the snack areas on different floors. We knew if we just started one or two, they'd simply put

78

them out and not evacuate. So, Hank dropped lit cigarettes in eight snack areas," Dana said. "I was right, by the way. No real risk."

She showed me an article on her cellphone about the hospital fires. And that's all the story was about—the arson perpetrated by a "young person wearing a hoodie." There was no mention of a forty-something who had escaped or even been treated at the hospital in the first place. I shook my head, still in disbelief.

"I don't know how I can ever repay you," I told her.

"Tell me your secret," she joked.

"I wish I knew."

She raised her eyebrows at that and stood up to head outside the barn. "We should probably get back on the road soon. I'll let you enjoy your cereal while I pay our host."

Back on the road. To where? And did she mean together, or were they going to drop me off somewhere so we could go our separate ways for good this time? Those were the easy questions; the hardest one still troubled me. As the reality began to set in about my extended life, I found I was becoming even more obsessed with finding out the reason why. The internet offered no updated information. Yes, more people were living past forty. No, the medical establishment had no idea why.

A new faction had cropped up: the anti-agers. They believed this whole thing was a big hoax. Nobody was actually living past their expiration date; the media and government were just perpetuating this lie. Why would they do that? According to these nuts, there were a host of possibilities. Stock market manipulation. Census conspiracies. A war on religion. When confronted with proof that people were living past expiration, the anti-agers refused to believe the facts. The scariest part was that while many anti-agers were who you might expect—the marginalized members of society—a significant number of them were people in positions of authority, from law enforcement to fringe medical professionals to elected officials.

I was listening to one such congressman spout off on a political podcast when I heard screaming outside the barn. I shuffled to the door and saw a group of angry people arguing with Dana and Hank. I was about to rush out there when someone yelled about calling the cops because of "that forty-something from the hospital." That made me duck back behind the barn door. *How did they find us?*

It didn't matter. The shouting grew louder and the debate more animated. Hank was scared. Dana held her arm around the boy, protecting him from the most vocal of the group, a hefty farmer wearing overalls and a green trucker hat. I grabbed a nearby shovel and considered my options. There were about half a dozen locals harassing my friends. Even if I hadn't just been in a car wreck, I would still be older and slower than every one of them.

I put down the shovel and stepped out of the barn. "Everything okay out here?" I asked with a smile. Predictably, my attempt to diffuse the situation didn't work.

* * *

Ten minutes later, I was sitting in the farmhouse living room on a couch next to Dana and Hank. We did not have a choice in the matter. The farmers were packed into the room, watching me intently. One of them, a gangly redhead with big teeth and a bigger scowl, stood near the door. He had a shotgun casually slung over his shoulder. The message was clear: I wasn't going anywhere, anytime soon.

"I thought you were good people when I asked to rent your barn," Dana snarled. "Guess I was wrong."

"Everyone's entitled to their opinion," the de facto leader of the group answered. He was a stocky guy in his mid-thirties. I assumed he was the leader because he talked the most. Everybody else just looked at me like a carnival attraction. "Where's Dale?"

"Should be here soon," a woman answered. "He was over in Clearwater with his daughter, selling a tractor. The man's going to work until the day he expires."

And with that comment, she glared at me. I was getting a bad feeling about this.

"The name's Luke," the stocky man said. "Is it true?"

I wanted to snark back and ask him if he wanted to know whether it was true that his name was Luke, but I bit my tongue.

"Well?" he prodded, his voice rising with anger.

I looked at Dana and her son. "Let them go," I told Luke. "They don't have anything to do with this."

"I asked you a question," he responded, his eyes trained on me.

"If you're asking about my age, then yes. It's true."

"He's lying!" the woman snarled.

"Fine, I'm lying," I said.

Luke nodded and motioned for folks to step out of the room. They grumbled but filed out. Other than Luke, only the redhead with the shotgun remained. Luke sat down in a recliner across from me. He regarded me for a few moments, then smiled. If I wasn't being held in his home against my will, I would've thought he was a genuinely affable fellow.

"I don't suppose you'll just come out and tell me," he said.

"Even if I knew what you were talking about, I'm not sure I

would," I answered.

"So, you don't know how you're post-forty, then?"

I sighed and shook my head. "Have you been watching the news? Nobody knows. Just because it's happening to me doesn't mean I have any idea why. I wish I fucking did."

"Well, the good news is even if we don't know why, we know you can help other people with your blood," he said.

I glanced at Dana. She grimaced back. I had to tread carefully.

"And how do we know that?" I asked.

"Shit, it's all over the web and radio. You have enough of those gene markers in one pint of your blood to help five people live past expiration," Luke explained in a way that made me realize just how detached from reality he was. "You haven't seen anything about it? Really?"

"It's possible we listen to different radio stations," I said.

Luke's demeanor changed as he took a harder look at me, trying to discern if I was lying. It seems we had stumbled deep into conspiracy theory territory. I suspected he was talking about some kind of fringe echo chamber where he kept being fed the same information from enough sources to make it seem like everyone in the country was talking about the same thing.

I figured the best way to combat one conspiracy theory was to throw out an even crazier one.

"You sure you want alien blood in those veins?" I countered.

"That's a bunch of horseshit," he said. "You're as human as the next guy. What? You really believe aliens came down and had sex with our ancestors? Maybe that's what some politicians want you to think."

So much for that approach.

Boots scraped against wood on the porch outside. The big guy guarding the door stepped aside and let an old man in. He had to be thirty-nine-plus, given his jowls and graying hair.

"Dale," Luke said, eyebrows raised.

Dale stopped a few feet from me and, like all the rest before him, inspected me for a few moments before speaking. If I somehow made it out of this alive, I was going to have to get used to being ogled at.

"We sure?" he asked Luke.

"I checked with Nancy at the hospital," Luke said. "This guy escaped and is 100 percent over forty. Says he doesn't know why. Claims he might be an alien."

Dale chuckled at that and looked at me with sympathy. "Ha! You been listening to too many of those doctors."

"Who else was I supposed to listen to?" I wondered aloud.

"He's mouthy. I can tamp that down if you want," Luke offered.

Dale was unbothered. For the first time, he looked at Dana and Hank.

"Let these two go," he said.

"You sure?" Luke asked, surprised.

"Did you read the article about their little escape? Setting fires in a hospital? She ain't going back to the authorities anytime soon," Dale said. He turned to Dana. "I hope it's obvious that if you try that shit again on our property, it'll be the last thing you ever do."

Dana looked at me, pained. She wanted to help but had her son to worry about. I nodded. I was on my own.

Chapter 16

Dale's wife Margie brought me some chocolate cake. It was the least she could do, she said. And she was right. Giving me a piece of cake after the local doctor drained a pint of my blood in her basement was indeed very close to the minimum of hospitality on Margie's part. If she wasn't careful, she'd be letting me eat regular meals too.

I guess I had to use the term *doctor* loosely, as the guy that drew my blood seemed more medical-adjacent than anything else. They called him "Doctor Tom," and it was my experience that anytime someone referred to a doctor by their first name, it wasn't a good sign.

"Get some rest," Doctor Tom said as he gathered his things to leave.

"I don't really have a choice, do I?" I responded. For the second time in as many days, I found myself secured to a bed. This go-round was zip ties, not handcuffs.

"Maybe next time it'll be rope," I joked aloud.

Doctor Tom left without responding, patting Dale on the shoulder as he left. Dale was resting in a beat-up recliner, watching the news. He'd just finished receiving the transfusion of my blood. No need to check for compatible blood types here!

That would've made way too much sense.

"Is it working yet?" I asked.

Dale frowned in my direction. "It's not instantaneous."

"Obviously."

"Look, Bill, there are two ways this can go," he said, before swigging from his beer bottle. "You can keep your attitude to yourself and give us some of your magic blood every couple days until we let you go. Or we can just decide to take whatever we can get all at once and be done with it. Given the whole situation, you might be more damn appreciative that I convinced Luke and the others to go the first route."

I was beginning to wish Dana hadn't busted me out of the hospital. At least with the ETF, I would have had a shot at humane treatment. With these folks, I gave my odds of survival about one in ten, given my lifelong inability to keep my attitude to myself.

Dana apologized a dozen times before she left, but it was the right call for her and Hank. I didn't expect to see her again. Even if I got out of this fucked-up situation, who knows how long I had left? I could still expire any minute. It's not like living past forty meant I was going to make it to fifty or anything. I also had to remind myself that despite one night of above-average sex and a few days together in the car, we didn't really know each other.

"Oh, shit!" Dale yelled, turning up the volume on the fairly obscure twenty-four-hour news channel.

"What now? You're supposed to drink my blood instead of injecting it?" I blurted, unable to control my snark.

Dale didn't even flinch. He was glued to the footage of a large, conical spacecraft hovering over what looked to be New York. I would've dismissed it as more fringe craziness, but the footage was crisp and incredible. The thing must have been the size of a football field, inverted and floating a few hundred feet above the ground in Brooklyn, according to the anchor.

"We are getting reports of similar craft in cities across the nation and the world," the anchor said, before detailing that the shiny spaceships appeared simultaneously about twenty minutes earlier. The dynamic of captor and captive disintegrated for a few moments as Dale and I looked at each other in disbelief.

"It was aliens after all," he said.

I had no witty retort to that. I was too busy trying to figure out what the hell it meant. Was I an alien? Was my ancestor an alien? Or was it just the biggest coincidence in the history of the world that spontaneous evolution and first contact happened in the same month?

Margie and Luke hurried into the room, just as anxious and shocked as we were. Margie knelt next to her husband and grabbed his hand. Luke just took a long pull from a bottle of whiskey.

"They blow anything up yet?" he asked.

"Shhhh … don't even say that!" Margie cried.

"Everybody shut up," Dale ordered, setting the TV to maximum volume.

"They have not attempted to make contact … or responded to our attempts … and have also not shown any signs of aggression as of yet. It's obviously a developing situation … and uh, we are dealing with real-time changes," the anchor reported, trying to rise to the moment but sputtering his words just the same. "Hold on, something seems to be happening now. Yes, it looks like a hatch is opening. We don't know if this is going on at every location or just with our feed … no I'm being told it's happening everywhere. Wow ..."

"Little green men. Twenty bucks!" Luke howled, growing increasingly volatile and drunk, before looking back at me with a menacing glare. "You better not be one of them."

Before I could respond, we all turned our attention back to the ship on the television. A figure was moving through the door and onto a small platform that had extended from the front panel of the craft.

"Well, I'll be a son of a bitch," Dale said. "It's one of us."

Indeed, the figure stepping out was not green at all. It didn't have big black eyes or a large head on top of a spindly alien body. It was just a guy. A handsome guy, in fact. He looked vaguely Mediterranean. Just then, the broadcast went multiscreen, and we saw three more ships, each with another generally normal-looking person standing on the platform. Two were men. Two were women.

"They certainly are good looking ..." Margie said.

"I'd tap that one in Australia," Luke said, reacting to the tall brunette on the feed from Sydney.

"Old," I said.

Two of them had gray hair. Despite the hair discoloration and some wrinkles, they seemed to be healthy overall. But they were definitely forty-somethings. Maybe even fifty-somethings. Though there was no way to really tell what a fifty-something would look like. The video snapped back to just our handsome fifty-something in Brooklyn. He smiled at the people amassed below the sprawling craft.

"I believe this is where I say we've come in peace?" he joked in perfect English. "But I guess that would be cliché."

I snorted a laugh. Of all the opening lines, sure, that's the one he went with.

"I'll also say it's good to be back, though none of you even knew we existed until this very moment," he said. "The truth is, we were here first. Nearly a million years ago. But we're not going to hold it against you. Quite the opposite, actually—we've come back to see that our little experiment is working."

It was hard to process. They were human. And they inhabited Earth before us. And modern-day humans were their experiment? Or just people like me were their experiment?

"You see, when we left the planet, there were only a few hundred thousand of us. Our technology was, how to put this gently, slightly more mature than yours. As was our age. We typically lived to seventy or eighty years, given the right environmental factors. Which is why for the past few millennia, we've been puzzled to notice that humanity's newest incarnation was similar to us in almost every way—save one. You people kept dying at exactly the same age. Strange! What an odd evolutionary quirk, we thought. And unfair. Even if you turned into a petty and violent race overall, there were still plenty of 'good oranges,' as you like to say."

He took a moment to recalibrate.

"Rather, apples. Good apples. We couldn't bear to think that our distant cousins on Earth were fated to die at just 14,610 solar days. So, about forty years ago, we flipped the switch. For a select few; 14,610 people to be exact. We thought it was symbolic."

The other people in the basement turned my way. Unlike before, when I was a curiosity or resource to be tapped, I was now something different. A liability. A danger. Maybe even an alien. And there were only 14,610 of us in the entire world.

Dale stiffened. If we were in a cartoon, a giant light bulb would have appeared over his head to go with his frightened expression. He didn't have to say a word for me to know that it just dawned on him that he might have just injected himself with alien blood.

The dude on TV continued. "While we assumed this gift would be met with celebration, it was not. Instead, the forty-somethings, as you call them, have been poked, prodded, and studied. They've been detained. In some cases, they've been killed."

Again, Dale's eyes fell on me with a mix of concern and regret. Luke tapped the butt of the gun in his belt. He was drunk and confused, which was never a good combination.

"So, our offer is simple. Leave these lucky individuals alone. Stop harassing them, or nobody else gets to live past forty ever again. You have one day to think about it. Oh, and in the meantime, we're taking the forty-somethings back."

And with that, he snapped his fingers.

Chapter 17

I woke up in a soft bed this time. My hands were secured with rope.

"Are you fucking kidding me?" I barked at nobody in particular.

"I told you he wouldn't think it's funny," someone said.

I looked over and saw the alien guy from the TV standing next to a teenager. She was wearing the same style of monochromatic gray bodysuit as he was. I was in a bland room with just a bed in the middle of it. The girl approached and started to remove the ropes.

"Sorry, he doesn't understand Earthlings at all," she said.

"Yes, it seems I've misjudged the situation," he admitted. "I thought you would find it humorous to have the very item restraining you—old-fashioned rope—that you surmised might be the next way someone secured you to a bed."

"Ah," I replied. "So, you can read our minds too?"

"Of course not. Don't be hyperbolic. We have an audio transponder embedded in your vocal cords."

I didn't even bother to question or consider that. I filed it away for a freak out in the near future.

"Where am I?" I asked instead.

"On a spaceship!" the teen cheerfully exclaimed.

"Oh. Cool?" I replied.

"See?" she said, turning to the silver-haired alien. "That's how you please an Earthling."

"My name is Greg," he said. "This is Valerie. We've teleported you here for your own safety. Hope you don't mind. Luke was about to shoot you."

"No, I guess I should thank you," I said, sitting up and stretching my back muscles. "For the help ... and the extra life."

"It was nothing, really," Greg boasted. "We just turned off a few genes on the day you were born. No biggie. Or no smallie? I'm still learning the slang."

"No biggie," I said.

"Good! I thought so. Anyway, we've got a couple dozen of your friends on this ship if you'd like to see them. Well, I say friends, but I really just mean compatriots. Other forty-somethings. A few of them didn't even know they were forty-somethings yet, so this was a double shock."

"Uh, okay, let's go see them."

"Valerie will take you," said Greg before exiting.

The teen looked at me with a smile that conveyed an equal mix of warmth and pity. I felt a bit like a puppy. "You've had a big couple of days," she said. "I was particularly interested in that escape you and your friends engineered. Very exciting. Want some burgers?"

* * *

The ship was everything I imagined an alien craft would be. Sterile, with white walls and floors. Flashing lights everywhere.

Then we got to the Wanda's.

Valerie led me into the fast-food establishment that had somehow been plopped right in the middle of the spacecraft. It was about twice the size of a normal Wanda's, but had all the same characteristics: booths, tables, the checkout lines, the kitchen in the back, and those square burgers. It also had just the right smell. Most of the seats were occupied by people in their late thirties (or very early forties) like me. They ran the gamut when it came to race and lifestyle. Most of them were dazed or chatting with others while they ate burgers and fries.

"Enjoy some food on us! I hear the Frosters are very good," Valerie said. "4153 will be giving a speech in about twenty minutes."

I looked at her with a confused expression.

"Ah, sorry, Greg. We thought if we called each other by number, it might distress you. I'm 78172, in case you were wondering."

78172, aka Valerie, spun on her heel and exited the restaurant, leaving me to approach the counter. The whole situation was surreal. I scanned the menu board as a smiling alien (I assume) waited for my order. A few minutes later, I was sitting at a booth with a bookkeeper from Utah. Beverly. She was a smart woman who was clearly rattled by being abducted by aliens. By comparison, I was perfectly sublime, which spoke volumes about how frazzled she was.

"This is beyond strange," she said. "Normal strange would be the fact that I turned forty two days ago. That's statistically abnormal and strange. Normal strange. But sitting on a spaceship eating what I hope is real cow from a fake Wanda's? That's beyond normal. We're in absurd territory."

"I agree," I said, not sure what else to say to the woman. I just dipped another fry in my Froster and nodded.

"Did you know you were different?" Beverly asked.

"Like … my whole life? Or just recently?"

"I knew. Ever since I was a kid, I was fascinated by the stars. I own three telescopes. Three. That's no coincidence, Ben."

"It's Bill. I never owned a telescope, but I was always interested in sci-fi movies. So, I guess you could say I had a connection with extraterrestrial notions."

"It's not the same," Beverly said, a little too harshly. "Sorry, I don't mean to minimize your experience."

"We're all on edge; don't worry about it," I said, looking for a way out. "I need some ketchup. You want anything?"

She shook her head, and I walked over to grab a few packets of ketchup. Then I found a seat by myself. I wasn't in the mood to talk to other people who were even more anxious than me.

* * *

If Greg's speech was supposed to make us feel better, it failed. Apparently, he thought that letting us know they could hear every word we said (I knew that already!) and monitor our whereabouts would put us at ease. I guess our words were heard but not always understood. They also had conquered the obstacles of teleportation, having plucked each and every one of us from Earth before zapping us here onto this ship.

"You may be wondering why we did all this," Greg said. "The answer is simple! Because your lives are too short by half. We don't know when or why you evolved to have such inadequate lifespans, but forty years simply isn't enough."

Inadequate lifespans. That was an interesting phrase. It suggested something was wrong with expiring at 14,610 days.

I looked around the room and could tell I wasn't the only one who had been harboring that feeling in their gut.

"So, why not just change everybody at the same time?" a man asked them between bites of his burger.

"We're advanced, but altering the genes of billions of people at the same time is still beyond our reach. We also wanted to test out what would happen. So far, we're not impressed," said Greg.

"He means to say not impressed with your fellow Earthlings!" Valerie chimed in. "We had not fully anticipated such a negative response from the rest of humanity. As you can see, we brought you here to keep you safe."

"You abducted us for our own good? And you think that won't make us even more feared after you drop us back into our lives?" I found myself blurting out.

"Uh … Greg?" Valerie handed that hot potato back to the older alien.

"It will all be just fine. What we know for sure is that people want to live longer! And we can make that happen in an orderly fashion," Greg said. But he was losing the crowd. My question had prompted similar shouts and criticisms. Soon Greg and Valerie's voices were lost in a sea of angry yells from us Earthlings.

Chapter 18

Over the next twelve hours, I ate at Wanda's two more times, watched a double feature in the spaceship's movie theater, and did my best to avoid the other people on board. They were either too friendly or too freaked out.

You'd think being on an alien ship would excite me, but it was fairly boring after the initial shock. Once Greg and Valerie stopped providing answers that mattered, there wasn't much else to do besides kill time before going back to Earth. Other than having the ability to completely alter our genes, these highly evolved versions of us were just as hapless as we were. Their "plan" consisted of telling the world anyone over forty was basically some sort of alien and then hoping it all would work out. When pressed on whether they'd give humanity the secret to unlocking our life-limiting DNA, Greg was noncommittal.

"It's not clear yet," he said.

On top of that, they forgot to add toilets that could handle solid waste. Apparently, our distant cousins eliminated solely via liquids. I was waiting in line for them to finish installing a proper toilet when Greg sidled up to me. "Bill, I was hoping for a word."

We stepped away from the crowd, and he forced a smile.

"I'll start by admitting we may not have fully considered our strategy," he said.

"You mean the part where you painted targets on our backs?" I asked.

"Yes, that part." He grimaced. "Which is why I wanted to ask if you had any ideas about how to limit the damage. You seem like one of the more reasonable people we picked up."

"What about the people on the other ships?"

"My counterparts are having similar discussions on those ships as well."

While I was glad Greg and his kind were at least owning up to their mistake, I wasn't quite sure what I could offer in the way of solutions.

"Have you mastered time travel?" I joked.

"Alas, no," he answered seriously.

"What about memory wipes?"

"Not on a massive scale like this," Greg said.

"I think the best way to help us would be to find a way to give everyone on Earth the ability to live past forty."

"That would take generations," Greg said. "And we're still not sure it's right for humanity."

"What the hell does that mean?" I asked. "It's not your decision to make."

"Actually, it's not. By conducting this experiment, we were getting in the way of nature," he reminded me. "And exactly which part of humanity's response to the possibility of extended life do you think warrants widespread adoption? If we hadn't extracted you, you'd still be giving your blood to those crazies down there."

He had me there. The simple fact a few people lived past their expiration date had indeed caused mass upheaval across the globe. Riots, financial crashes and kidnappings aren't the hallmarks of a civilized response.

"Short of giving everyone a longer life, do you have any ideas?" Greg asked.

* * *

The place was nice. It had two bedrooms, a big backyard, and even one of those oversized fridges in the kitchen. I stood in the living room, considering the color of the walls—yellow, that would certainly have to be changed—and realized for the first time in years, I was a free man. I was not locked to a particular destiny. I wasn't even locked to my old name. Moving forward, I would be known as Paul Remington. It made me feel like a secret agent. Mr. Remington.

I had $100,000 in the bank and a Subaru in the driveway.

It's funny—people aspire to be famous and celebrated for their uniqueness, but the best thing you can be when you're special is anonymous. Just as I was starting to feel comfortable, I saw two figures approaching the front door. One was tall. The other was short. Langdon and Jones. I opened the door before they had a chance to knock.

"Mr. Remington," Langdon quipped.

If I didn't know better, I'd say he wasn't upset at all. He had no choice but to acknowledge my new identity; it was his very department that gave it to me. A week earlier, his job was to track me down and detain me. Now, thanks to the deal struck between the government and Greg's alien friends, he was tasked with protecting me.

"Come on in, guys," I said, trying to be congenial. "Can I get either of you a beer?"

"We're good," Jones said, not moving from the porch. He wasn't hiding his contempt as well as his partner.

"Just came by to see how things are going with the new, well, everything," Langdon said.

"I've been here all of five minutes, but so far, so good."

"If you need anything, we're only a text or phone call away. The ETF takes your safety very seriously," Langdon said. He somehow did so with a straight face. It was impressive.

I nodded, and we all just stood there for a few moments.

"Is there anything else?" I asked.

"Do you have any idea how long you'll be staying here?" Jones asked.

He was fishing. I didn't bite.

"I guess you could say I'll be taking it one day at a time," I answered, before closing the door on the two field reps. I figured that would keep Jones gnashing his teeth for a few hours.

The truth was that I had no idea how long I'd be living at that house. Or living at all, for that matter. When Greg had asked me if I had any ideas for fixing their little fuck-up, I suggested something akin to the Witness Protection Program. Give any of us who wanted it a new identity and enough money to start a new life with whatever time we had left.

"Do you want to know how much time you have left?" Greg had asked me at the end of that conversation.

Something inside me yearned for that knowledge. I'd spent my whole life knowing exactly when it would end, and suddenly I was being given that choice again. I could've just rolled up in that warm blanket of certainty and told Greg to reveal just how long this new lease on life would last.

"You know the day?" I asked.

"I know roughly what your body is capable of," he had told

me. "Everyone is different. Barring a car accident or random act of violence, I could tell you what to expect within a year or so."

That's when it hit me. The answer was simple.

"Never tell anyone," I said to Greg. "No matter how many people you plan to give this gift to, don't tell us how long we have. A month. A year. Twenty years. We're better off not knowing. It's the only way this works."

"Maybe your people are ready after all," Greg had said in response to that.

I wasn't so sure I agreed with him, but that was the exciting part.

About the Author

George Ellis lives in Austin, where he writes science fiction books at night and runs an advertising agency by day. In addition to novels, he writes screenplays, viral videos and Internet memes.

Also by George Ellis

A teenage wrecker is forced to steal the hottest tech in the verse.

Wreckers
At 19 years old, Denver is the youngest wrecker in space. His only companion, other than his one-eyed cat, is an AI navigator based on classic 21st century sitcom personalities. That all changes when Denver meets Batista, a mechanic who claims to know what happened to Denver's missing father and brother. Soon, Denver is drawn into trouble with the various forces in the galaxy — bandits, feds and rival wreckers.